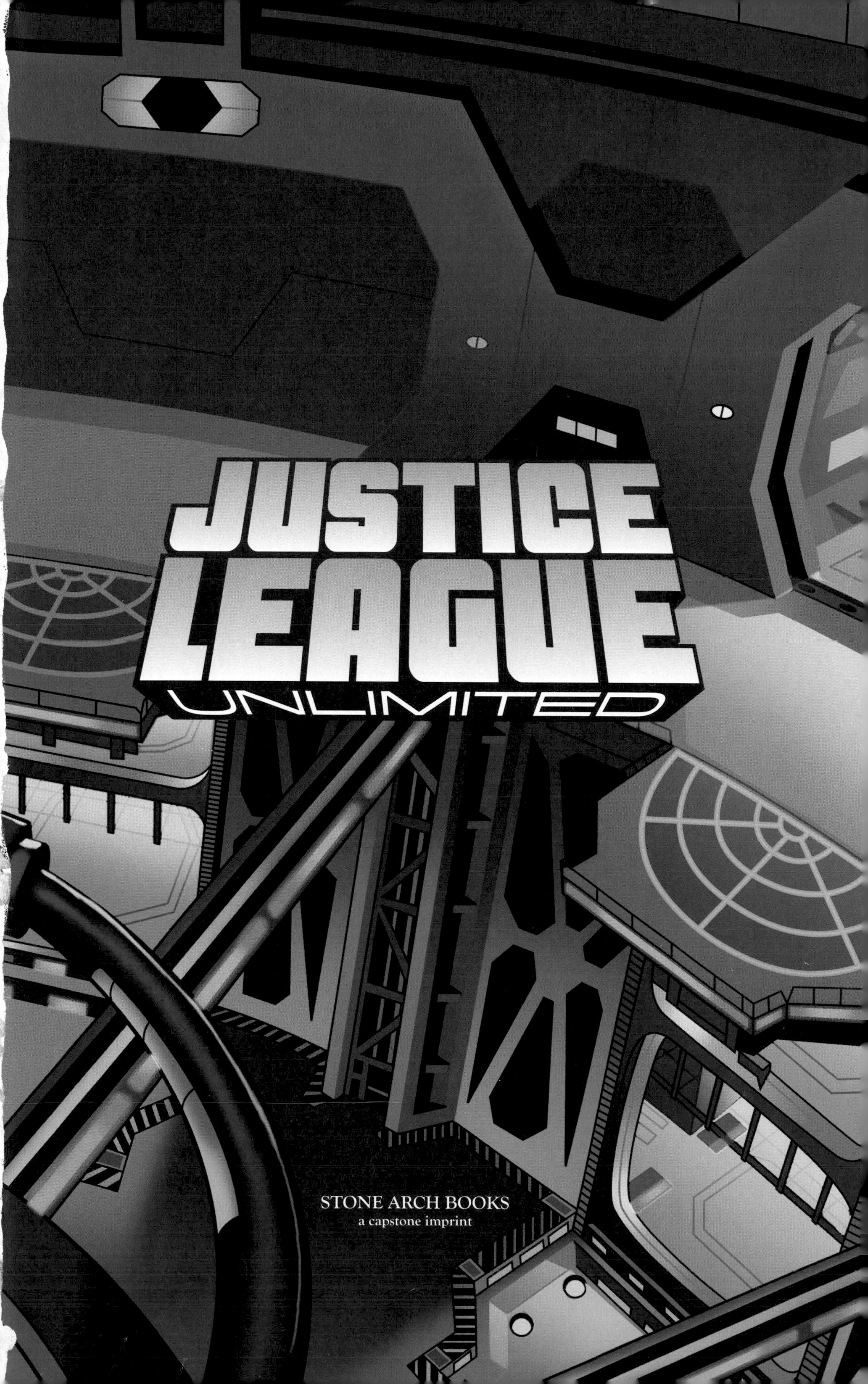

JUSTICE LEAGUE UNLIMITED

STONE ARCH BOOKS
a capstone imprint

STONE ARCH BOOKS™

Published in 2013
A Capstone Imprint
1710 Roe Crest Drive
North Mankato, MN 56003
www.capstonepub.com

Originally published by DC Comics in the U.S. in single
magazine form as Justice League Unlimited #6.
Copyright © 2013 DC Comics. All Rights Reserved.

DC Comics
1700 Broadway, New York, NY 10019
A Warner Bros. Entertainment Company

Printed in China by Nordica.
0413/CA21300442
032013   007226NORDF13

Cataloging-in-Publication Data is available
at the Library of Congress website:
ISBN: 978-1-4342-6042-0 (library binding)

Summary: John Stewart and Green Arrow
encounter an old member of the Green
Lantern Corps as they fight a trio of alien
invaders. Will this elderly Lantern be able
to help them defeat their foes, or is he too
out of touch with reality?

STONE ARCH BOOKS

Ashley C. Andersen Zantop *Publisher*
Michael Dahl *Editorial Director*
Sean Tulien & Donald Lemke *Editors*
Heather Kindseth *Creative Director*
Bob Lentz & Hilary Wacholz *Designers*
Kathy McColley *Production Specialist*

DC COMICS
Tom Palmer Jr. *Original U.S. Editor*

JUSTICE LEAGUE UNLIMITED

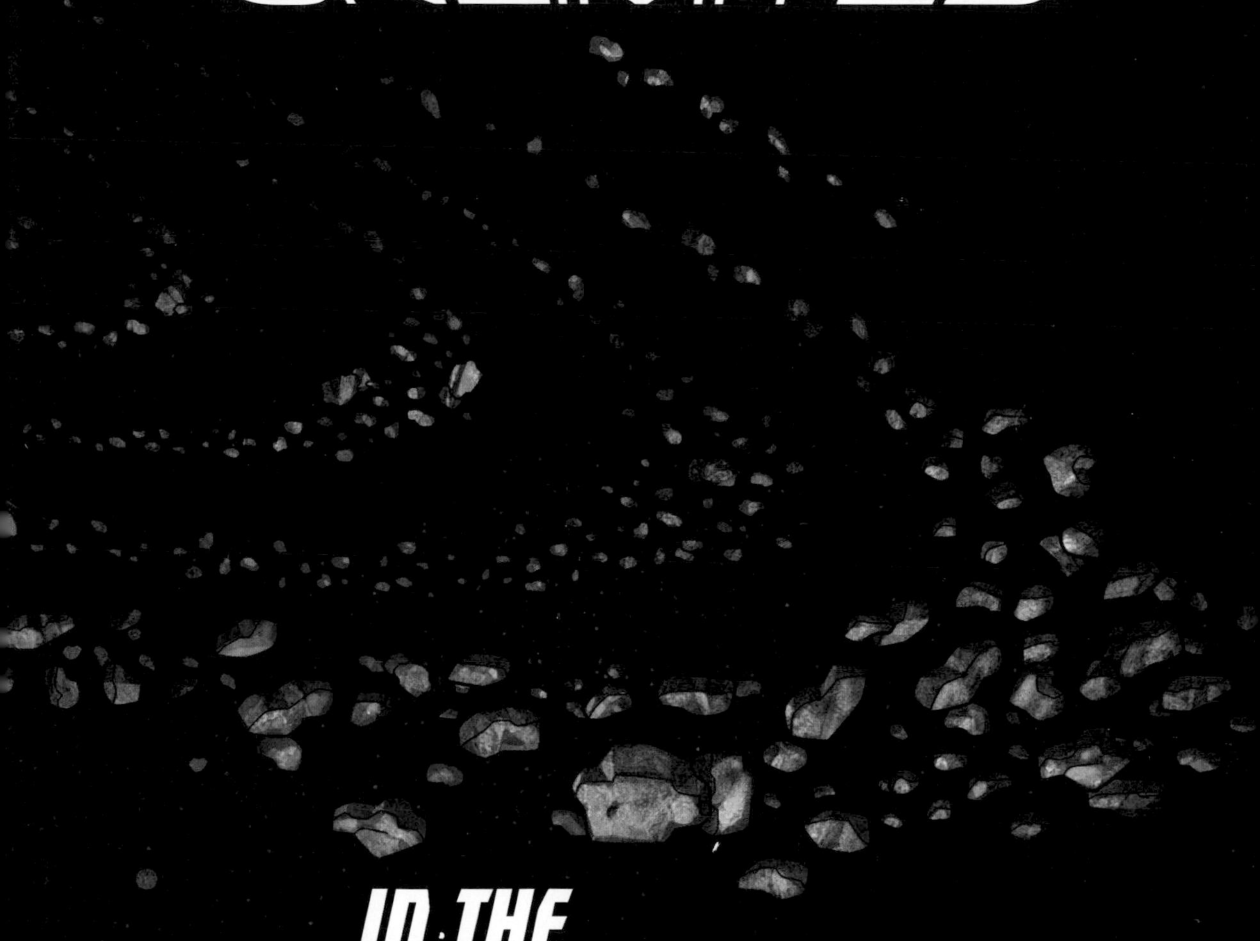

IN THE DIMMING LIGHT

Adam Beechen.. writer
Carlo Barberi & Walden Wong.................artists
Heroic Age ....colorist
Pat Brosseau...letterer

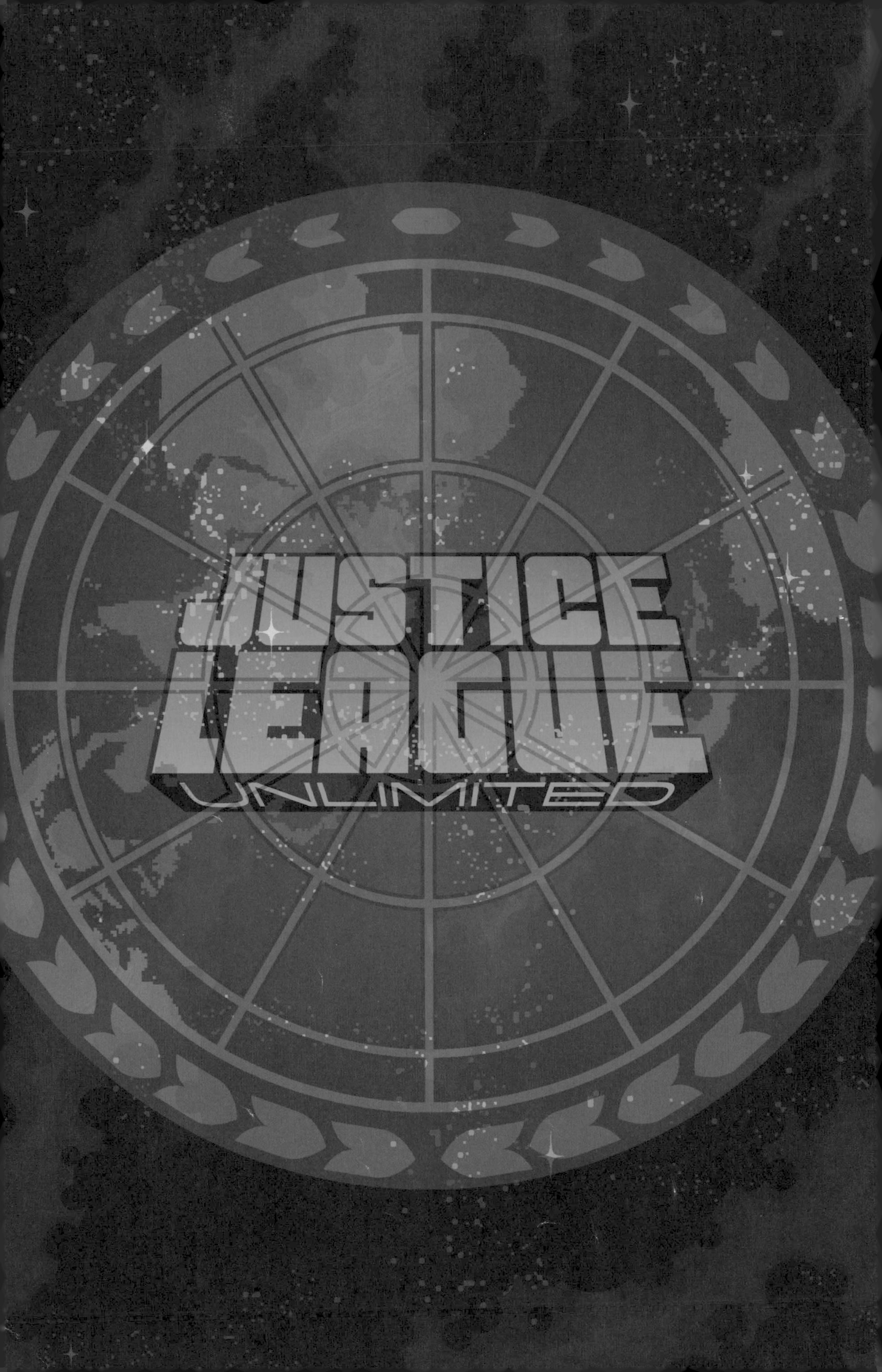
JUSTICE LEAGUE
UNLIMITED

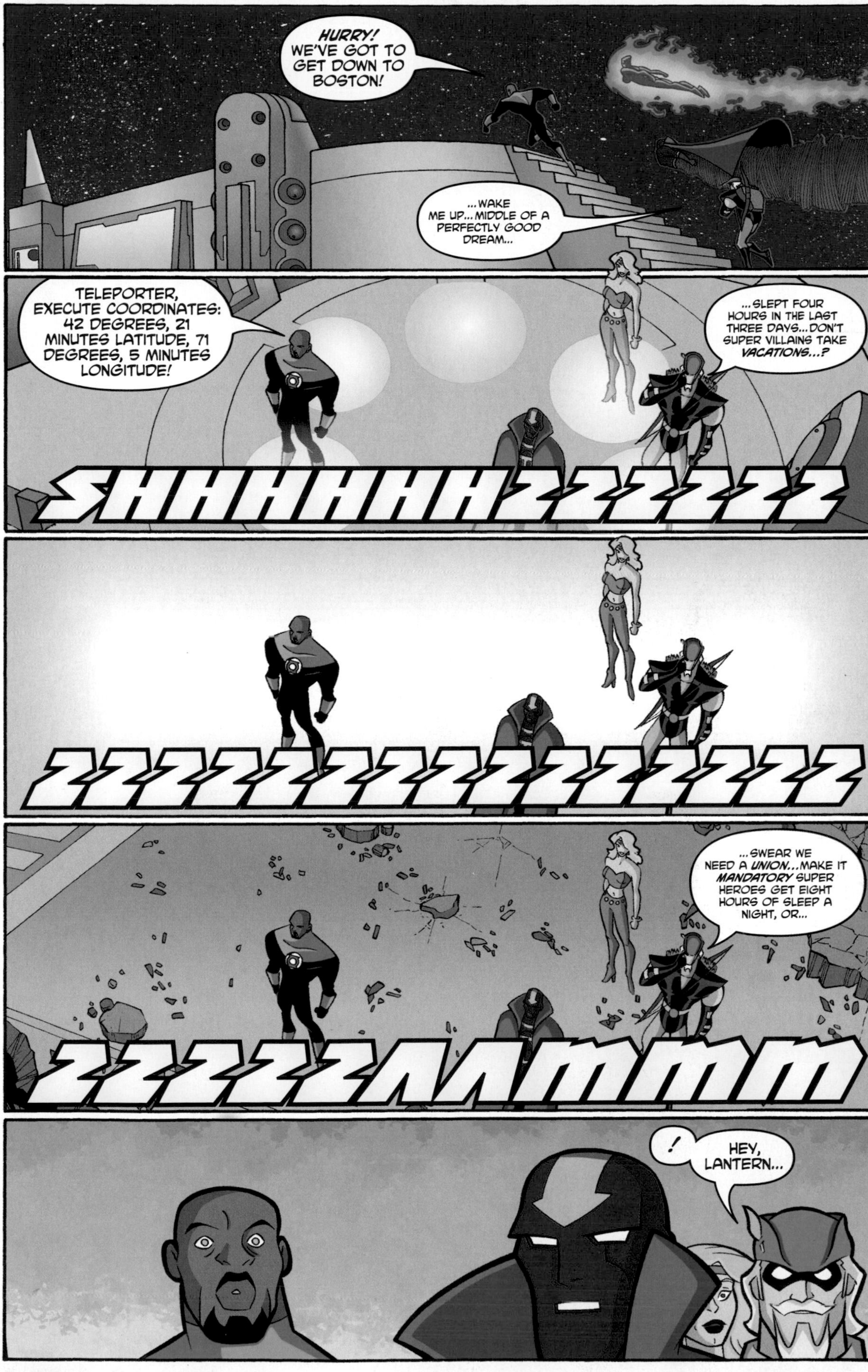
HURRY! WE'VE GOT TO GET DOWN TO BOSTON!
...WAKE ME UP...MIDDLE OF A PERFECTLY GOOD DREAM...
TELEPORTER, EXECUTE COORDINATES: 42 DEGREES, 21 MINUTES LATITUDE, 71 DEGREES, 5 MINUTES LONGITUDE!
...SLEPT FOUR HOURS IN THE LAST THREE DAYS...DON'T SUPER VILLAINS TAKE VACATIONS...?
SHHHHHHZZZZZZ
ZZZZZZZZZZZZZZZZZ
...SWEAR WE NEED A UNION...MAKE IT MANDATORY SUPER HEROES GET EIGHT HOURS OF SLEEP A NIGHT, OR...
ZZZZZAAMMMM
!
HEY, LANTERN...

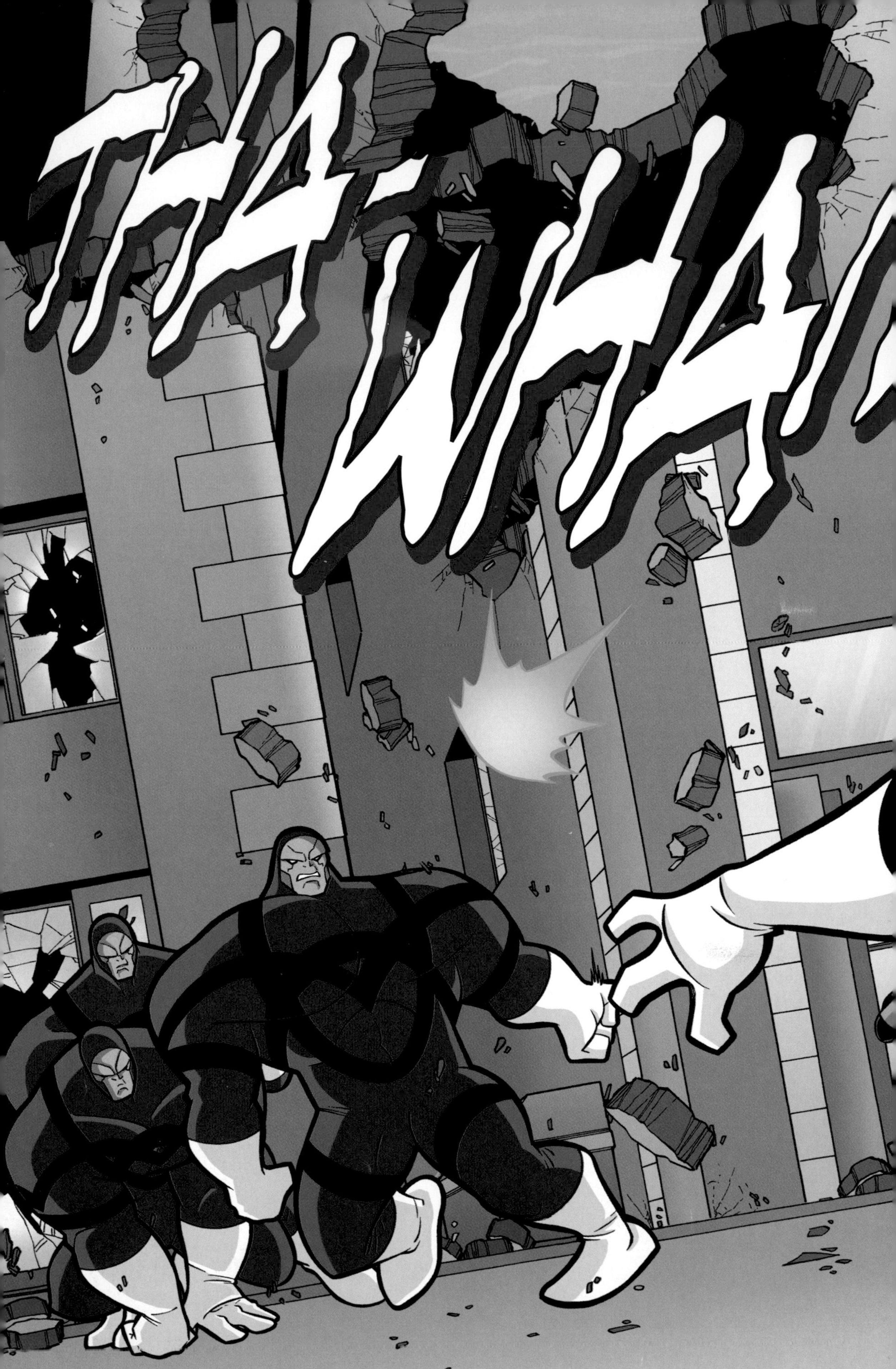
THA-WHAM

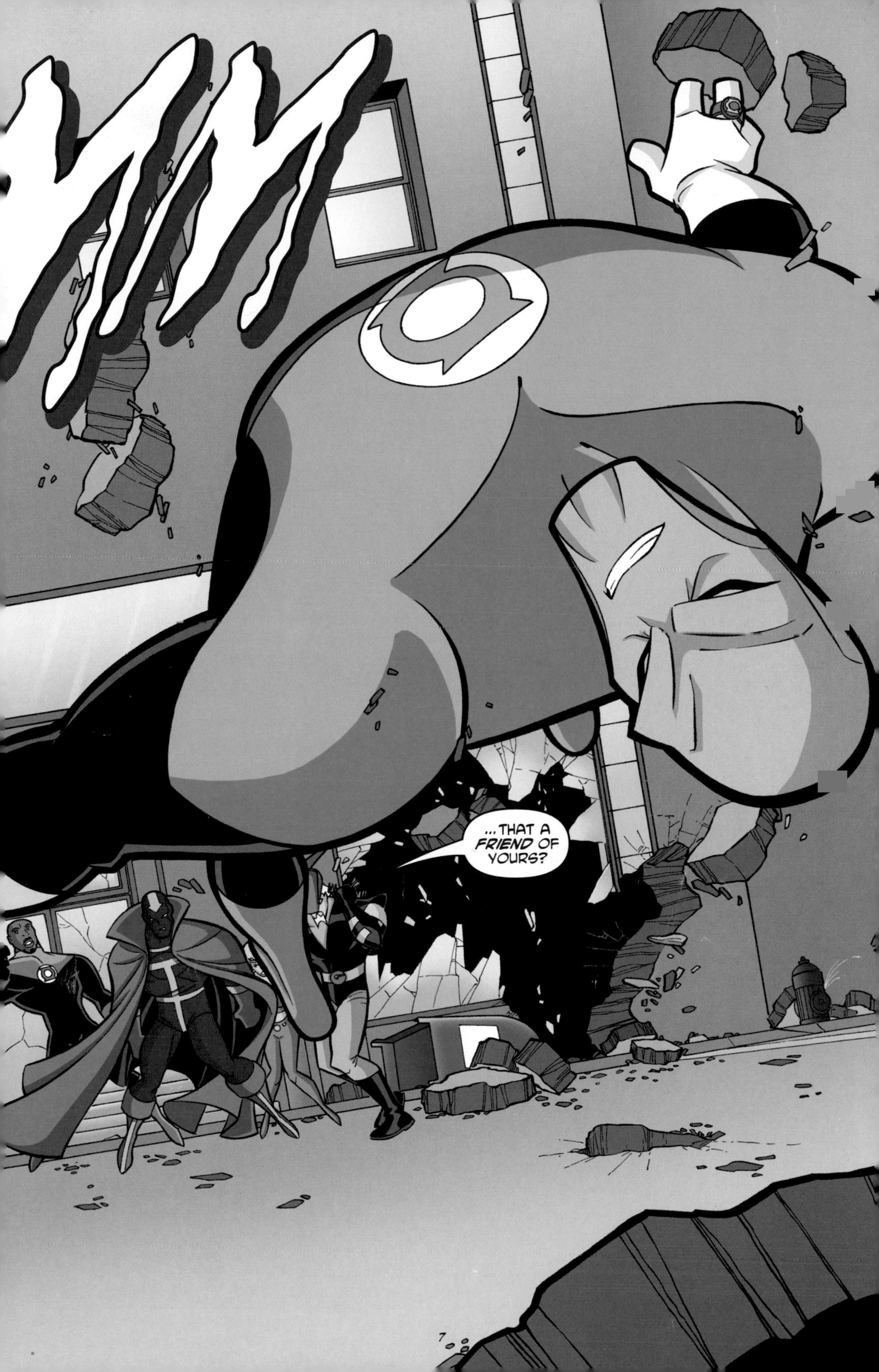
...THAT A FRIEND OF YOURS?

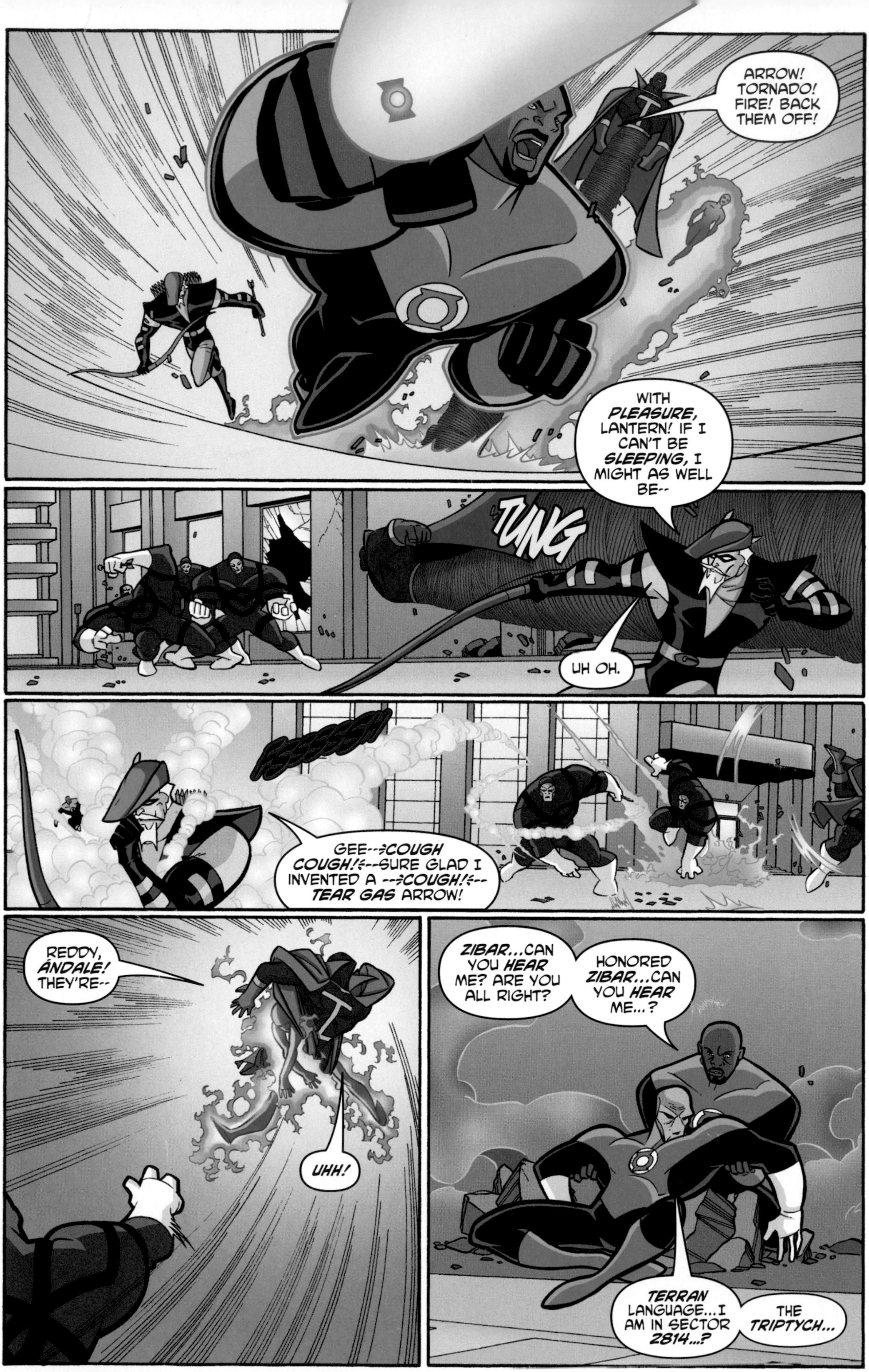
ARROW! TORNADO! FIRE! BACK THEM OFF!
WITH PLEASURE, LANTERN! IF I CAN'T BE SLEEPING, I MIGHT AS WELL BE--
TUNG
UH OH.
GEE--COUGH COUGH!--SURE GLAD I INVENTED A --COUGH!-- TEAR GAS ARROW!
REDDY, ÁNDALE! THEY'RE--
UHH!
ZIBAR...CAN YOU HEAR ME? ARE YOU ALL RIGHT?
HONORED ZIBAR...CAN YOU HEAR ME...?
TERRAN LANGUAGE...I AM IN SECTOR 2814...?
THE TRIPTYCH...

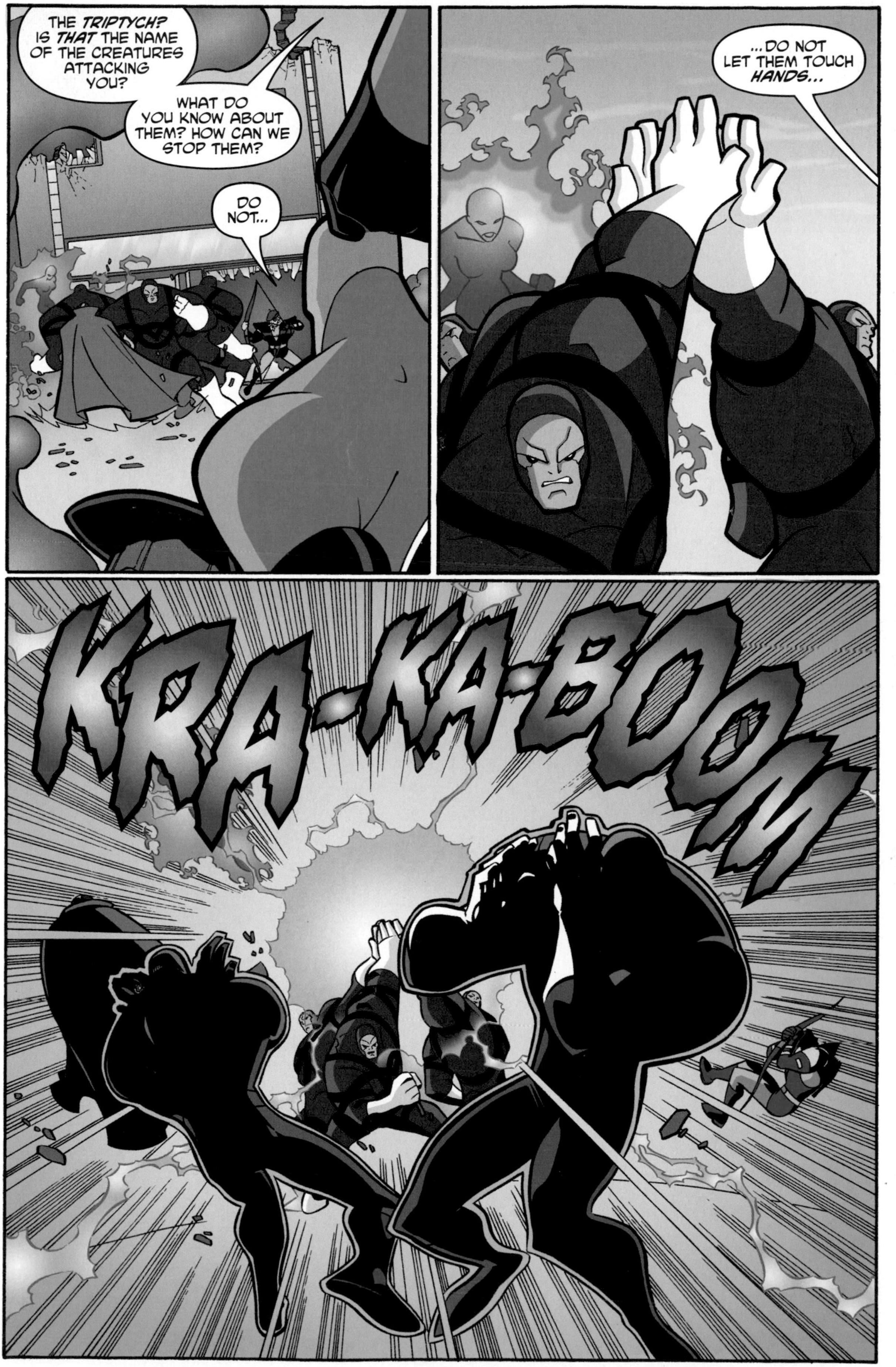
THE TRIPTYCH? IS THAT THE NAME OF THE CREATURES ATTACKING YOU?
WHAT DO YOU KNOW ABOUT THEM? HOW CAN WE STOP THEM?
DO NOT...
...DO NOT LET THEM TOUCH HANDS...
KRA-KA-BOOM

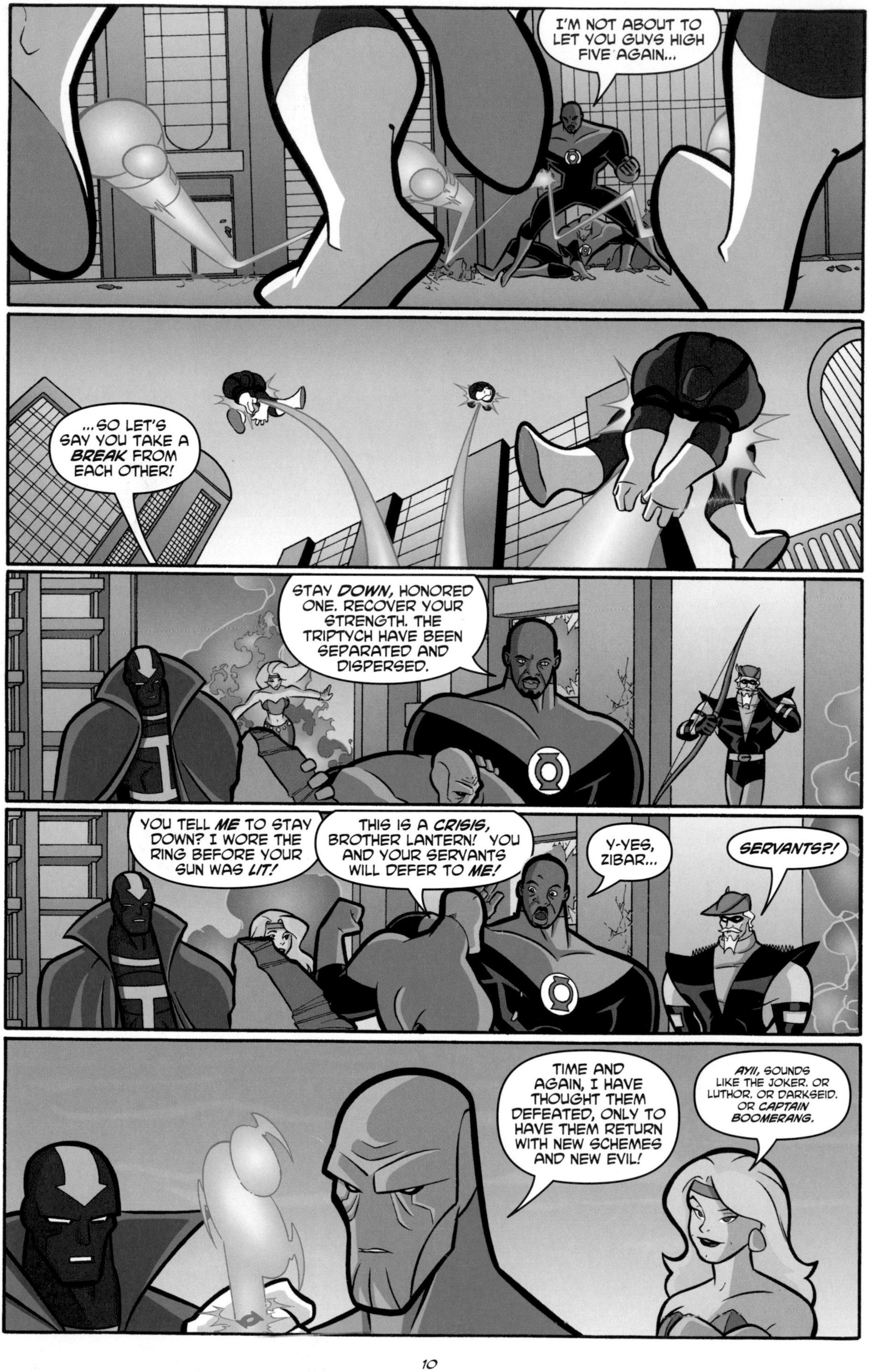
I'M NOT ABOUT TO LET YOU GUYS HIGH FIVE AGAIN...
...SO LET'S SAY YOU TAKE A *BREAK* FROM EACH OTHER!
STAY *DOWN,* HONORED ONE. RECOVER YOUR STRENGTH. THE TRIPTYCH HAVE BEEN SEPARATED AND DISPERSED.
YOU TELL *ME* TO STAY DOWN? I WORE THE RING BEFORE YOUR SUN WAS *LIT!*
THIS IS A *CRISIS,* BROTHER LANTERN! YOU AND YOUR SERVANTS WILL DEFER TO *ME!*
Y-YES, ZIBAR...
SERVANTS?!
TIME AND AGAIN, I HAVE THOUGHT THEM DEFEATED, ONLY TO HAVE THEM RETURN WITH NEW SCHEMES AND NEW EVIL!
AYII, SOUNDS LIKE THE JOKER. OR LUTHOR. OR DARKSEID. OR *CAPTAIN BOOMERANG.*

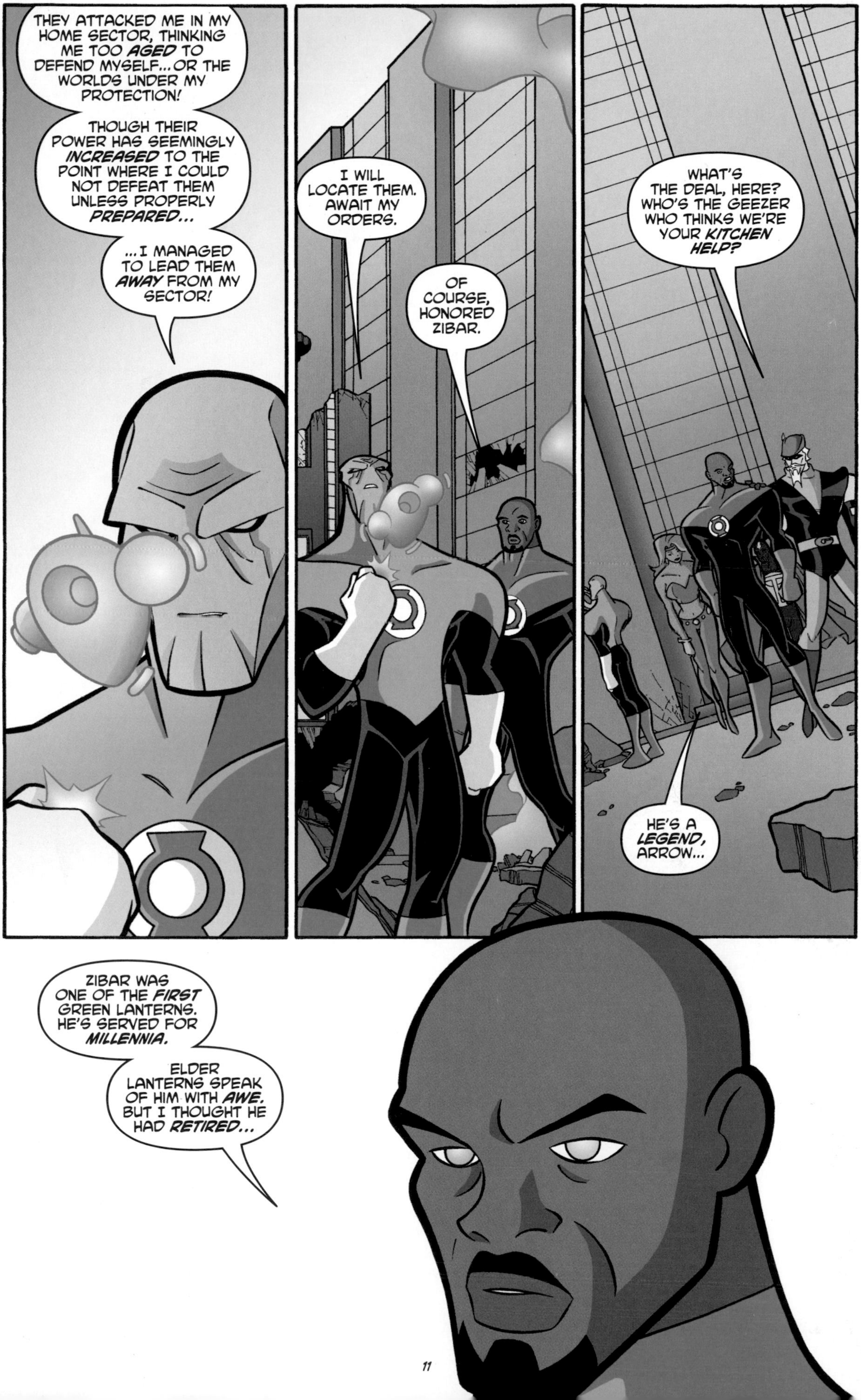
THEY ATTACKED ME IN MY HOME SECTOR, THINKING ME TOO AGED TO DEFEND MYSELF...OR THE WORLDS UNDER MY PROTECTION!
THOUGH THEIR POWER HAS SEEMINGLY INCREASED TO THE POINT WHERE I COULD NOT DEFEAT THEM UNLESS PROPERLY PREPARED...
...I MANAGED TO LEAD THEM AWAY FROM MY SECTOR!
I WILL LOCATE THEM. AWAIT MY ORDERS.
OF COURSE, HONORED ZIBAR.
WHAT'S THE DEAL, HERE? WHO'S THE GEEZER WHO THINKS WE'RE YOUR KITCHEN HELP?
HE'S A LEGEND, ARROW...
ZIBAR WAS ONE OF THE FIRST GREEN LANTERNS. HE'S SERVED FOR MILLENNIA.
ELDER LANTERNS SPEAK OF HIM WITH AWE. BUT I THOUGHT HE HAD RETIRED...

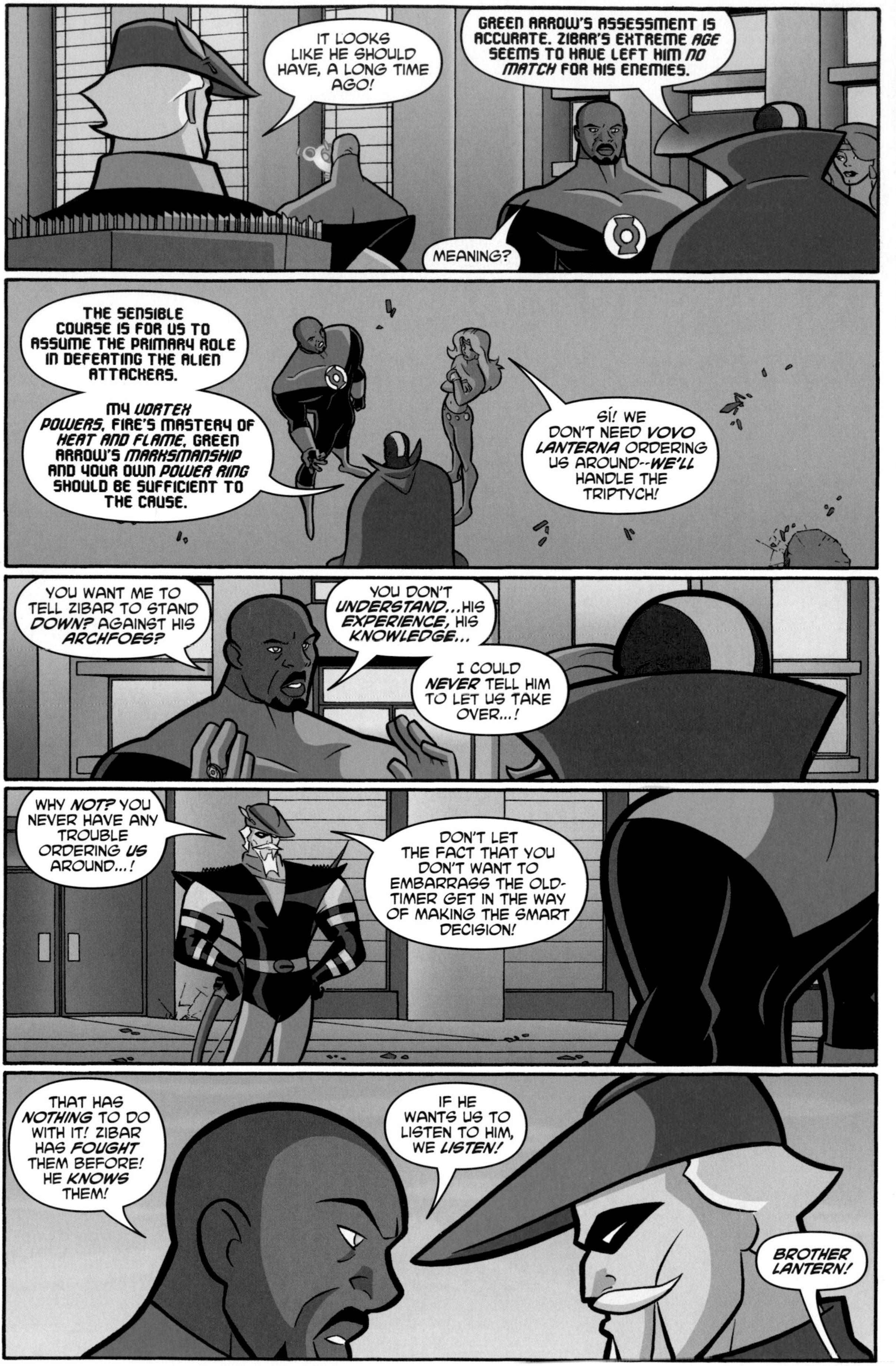
IT LOOKS LIKE HE SHOULD HAVE, A LONG TIME AGO!
GREEN ARROW'S ASSESSMENT IS ACCURATE. ZIBAR'S EXTREME *AGE* SEEMS TO HAVE LEFT HIM *NO MATCH* FOR HIS ENEMIES.
MEANING?
THE SENSIBLE COURSE IS FOR US TO ASSUME THE PRIMARY ROLE IN DEFEATING THE ALIEN ATTACKERS.
MY *VORTEX POWERS*, FIRE'S MASTERY OF *HEAT AND FLAME*, GREEN ARROW'S *MARKSMANSHIP* AND YOUR OWN *POWER RING* SHOULD BE SUFFICIENT TO THE CAUSE.
SÍ! WE DON'T NEED *VOVO LANTERNA* ORDERING US AROUND--*WE'LL* HANDLE THE TRIPTYCH!
YOU WANT ME TO TELL ZIBAR TO STAND *DOWN?* AGAINST HIS *ARCHFOES?*
YOU DON'T *UNDERSTAND*...HIS *EXPERIENCE*, HIS *KNOWLEDGE*...
I COULD *NEVER* TELL HIM TO LET US TAKE OVER...!
WHY *NOT?* YOU NEVER HAVE ANY TROUBLE ORDERING *US* AROUND...!
DON'T LET THE FACT THAT YOU DON'T WANT TO EMBARRASS THE OLD-TIMER GET IN THE WAY OF MAKING THE SMART DECISION!
THAT HAS *NOTHING* TO DO WITH IT! ZIBAR HAS *FOUGHT* THEM BEFORE! HE *KNOWS* THEM!
IF HE WANTS US TO LISTEN TO HIM, WE *LISTEN!*
BROTHER LANTERN!

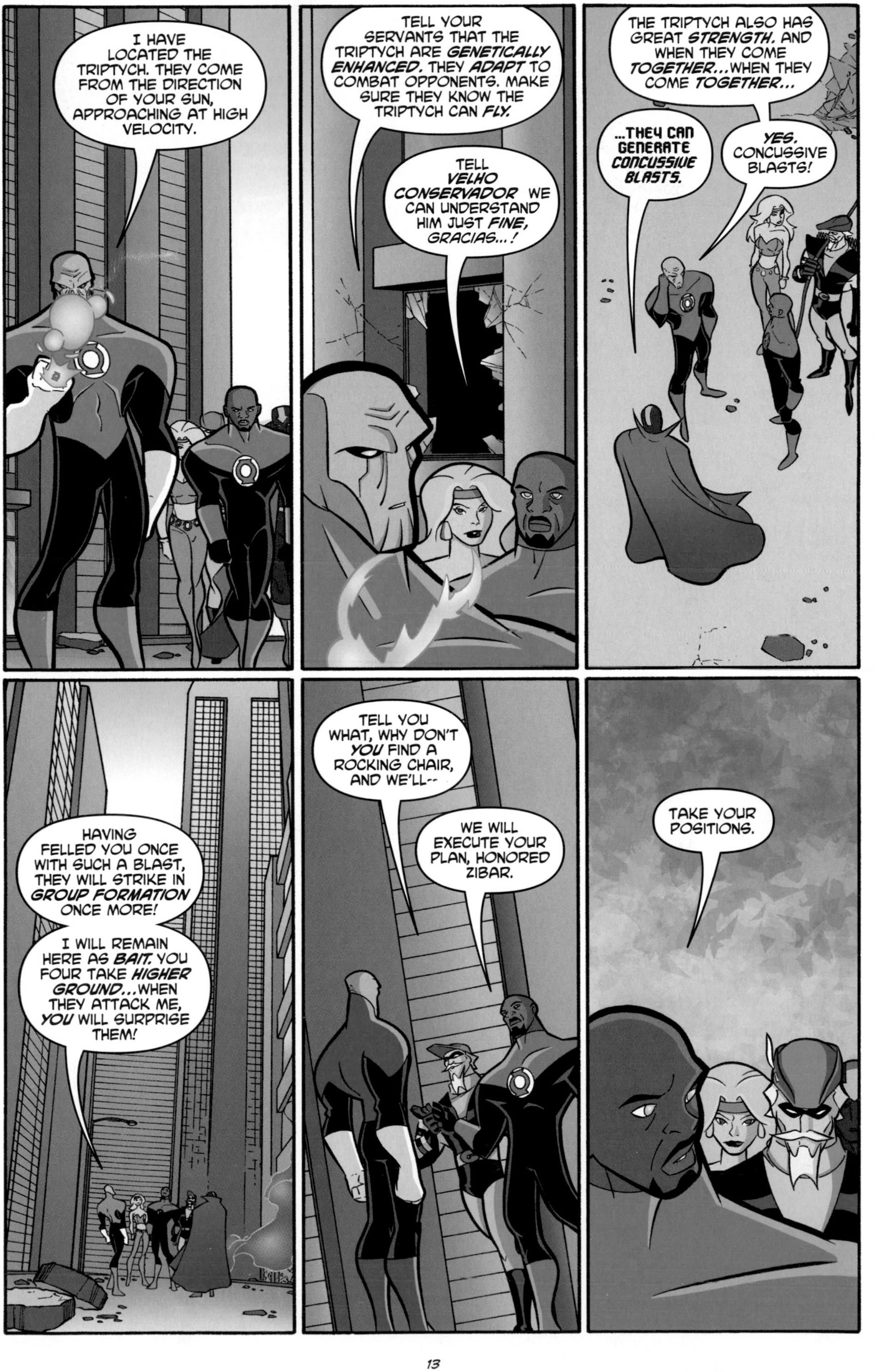
I HAVE LOCATED THE TRIPTYCH. THEY COME FROM THE DIRECTION OF YOUR SUN, APPROACHING AT HIGH VELOCITY.
TELL YOUR SERVANTS THAT THE TRIPTYCH ARE GENETICALLY ENHANCED. THEY ADAPT TO COMBAT OPPONENTS. MAKE SURE THEY KNOW THE TRIPTYCH CAN FLY.
TELL VELHO CONSERVADOR WE CAN UNDERSTAND HIM JUST FINE, GRACIAS...!
THE TRIPTYCH ALSO HAS GREAT STRENGTH. AND WHEN THEY COME TOGETHER...WHEN THEY COME TOGETHER...
...THEY CAN GENERATE CONCUSSIVE BLASTS.
YES. CONCUSSIVE BLASTS!
HAVING FELLED YOU ONCE WITH SUCH A BLAST, THEY WILL STRIKE IN GROUP FORMATION ONCE MORE!
I WILL REMAIN HERE AS BAIT. YOU FOUR TAKE HIGHER GROUND...WHEN THEY ATTACK ME, YOU WILL SURPRISE THEM!
TELL YOU WHAT, WHY DON'T YOU FIND A ROCKING CHAIR, AND WE'LL--
WE WILL EXECUTE YOUR PLAN, HONORED ZIBAR.
TAKE YOUR POSITIONS.

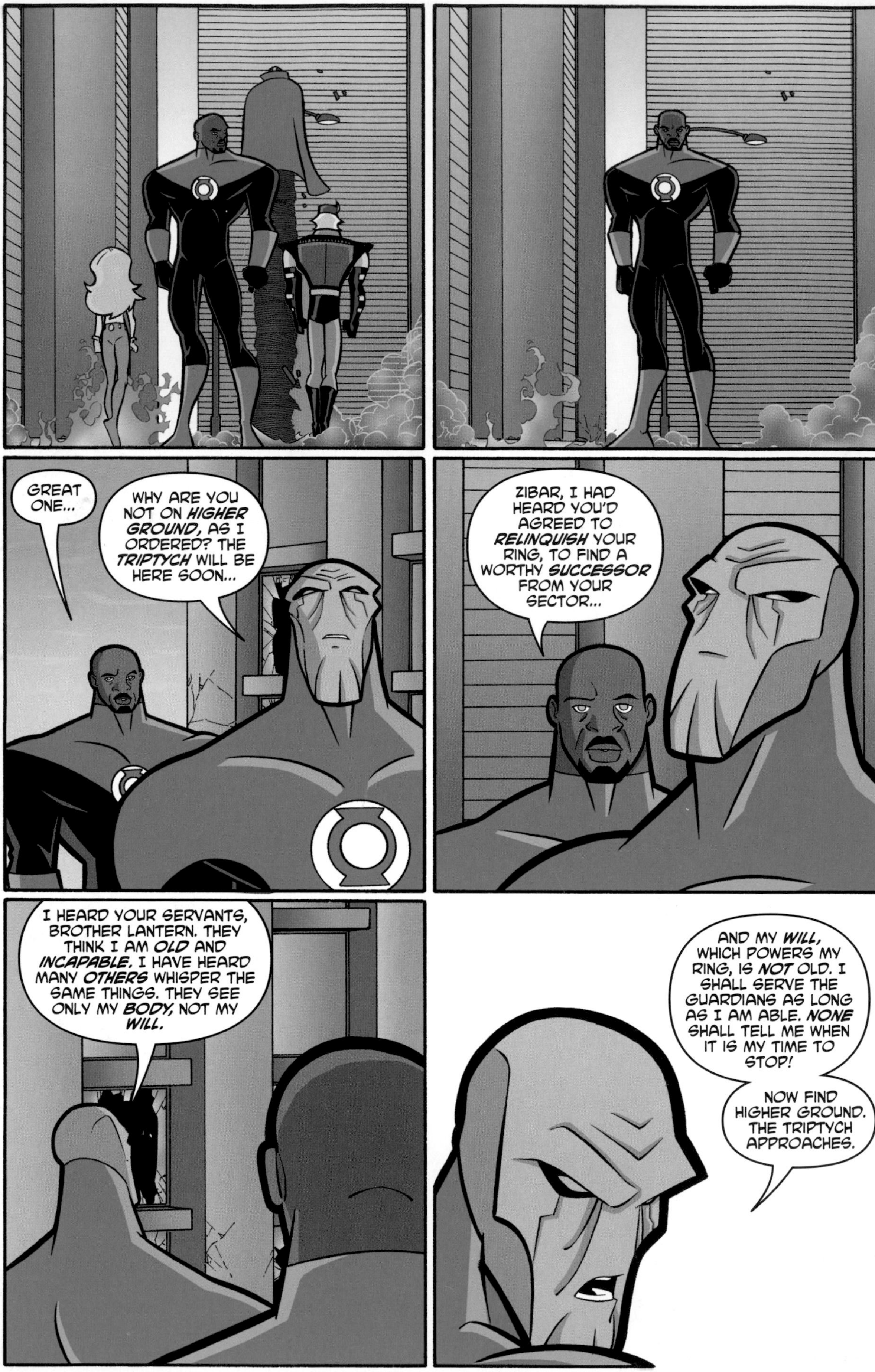
GREAT ONE...
WHY ARE YOU NOT ON HIGHER GROUND, AS I ORDERED? THE TRIPTYCH WILL BE HERE SOON...
ZIBAR, I HAD HEARD YOU'D AGREED TO RELINQUISH YOUR RING, TO FIND A WORTHY SUCCESSOR FROM YOUR SECTOR...
I HEARD YOUR SERVANTS, BROTHER LANTERN. THEY THINK I AM OLD AND INCAPABLE. I HAVE HEARD MANY OTHERS WHISPER THE SAME THINGS. THEY SEE ONLY MY BODY, NOT MY WILL.
AND MY WILL, WHICH POWERS MY RING, IS NOT OLD. I SHALL SERVE THE GUARDIANS AS LONG AS I AM ABLE. NONE SHALL TELL ME WHEN IT IS MY TIME TO STOP!
NOW FIND HIGHER GROUND. THE TRIPTYCH APPROACHES.

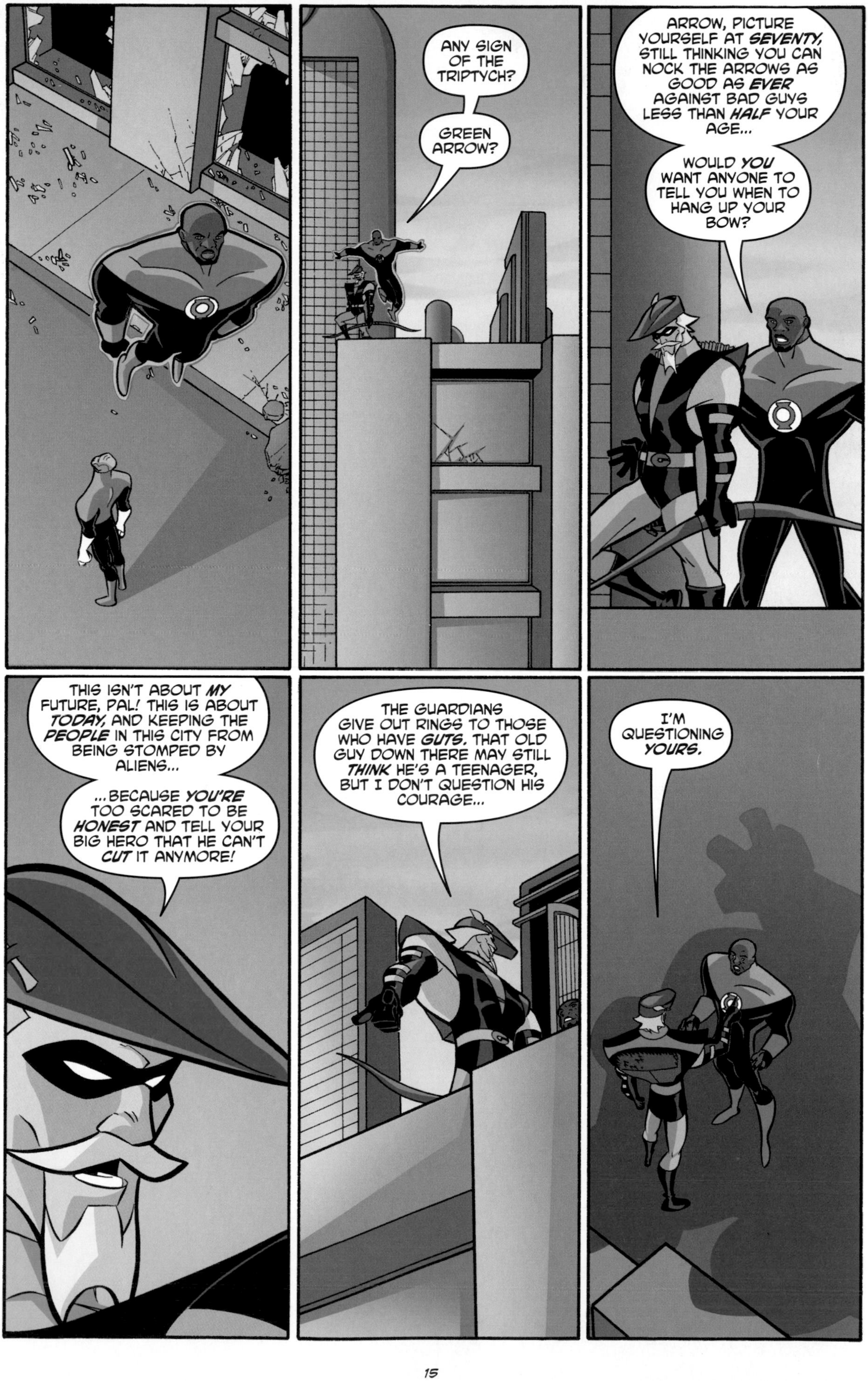
ANY SIGN OF THE TRIPTYCH?
GREEN ARROW?
ARROW, PICTURE YOURSELF AT SEVENTY, STILL THINKING YOU CAN NOCK THE ARROWS AS GOOD AS EVER AGAINST BAD GUYS LESS THAN HALF YOUR AGE...
WOULD YOU WANT ANYONE TO TELL YOU WHEN TO HANG UP YOUR BOW?
THIS ISN'T ABOUT MY FUTURE, PAL! THIS IS ABOUT TODAY, AND KEEPING THE PEOPLE IN THIS CITY FROM BEING STOMPED BY ALIENS...
...BECAUSE YOU'RE TOO SCARED TO BE HONEST AND TELL YOUR BIG HERO THAT HE CAN'T CUT IT ANYMORE!
THE GUARDIANS GIVE OUT RINGS TO THOSE WHO HAVE GUTS. THAT OLD GUY DOWN THERE MAY STILL THINK HE'S A TEENAGER, BUT I DON'T QUESTION HIS COURAGE...
I'M QUESTIONING YOURS.

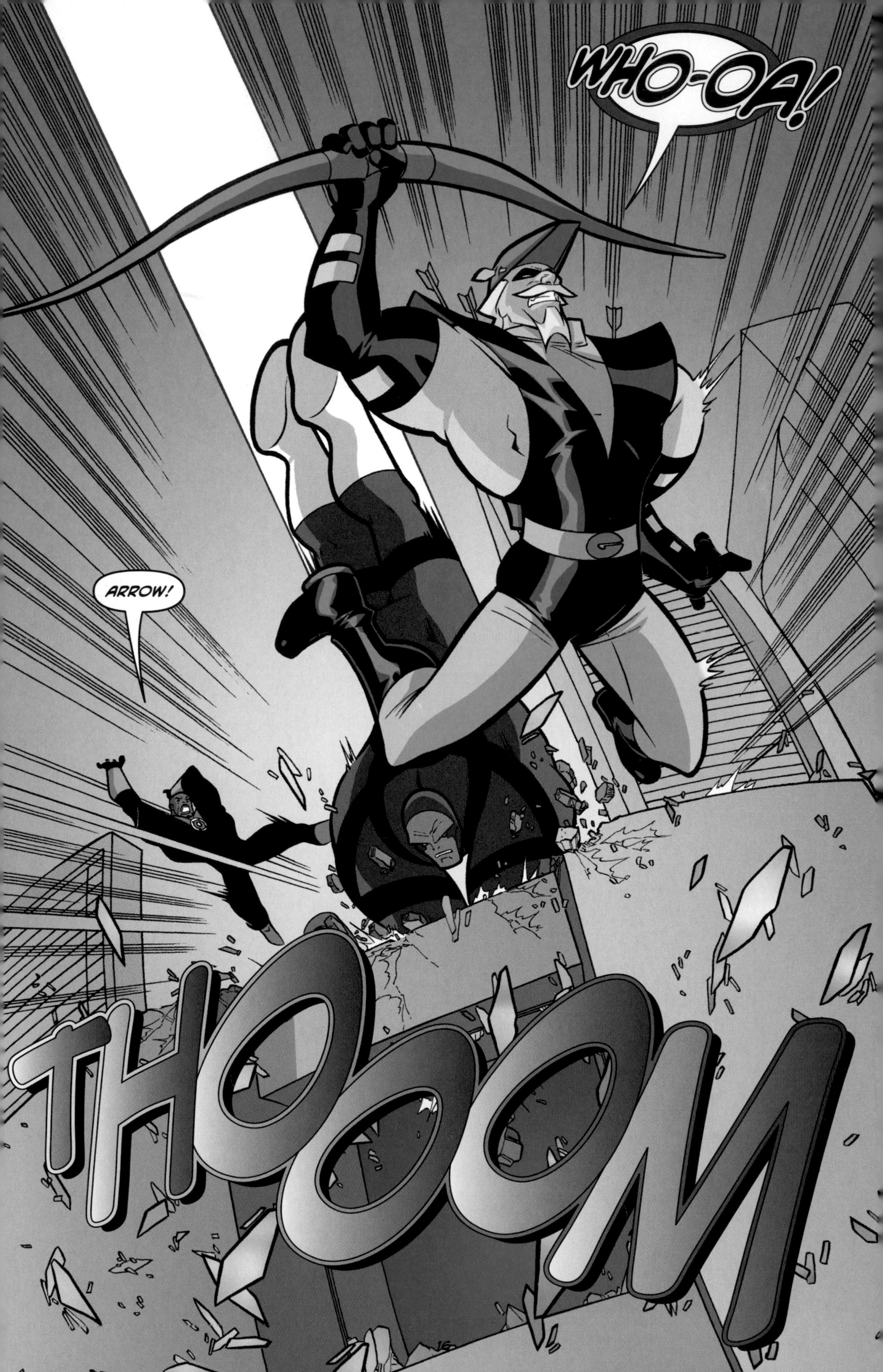
WHO-OA!
ARROW!
THOOOM

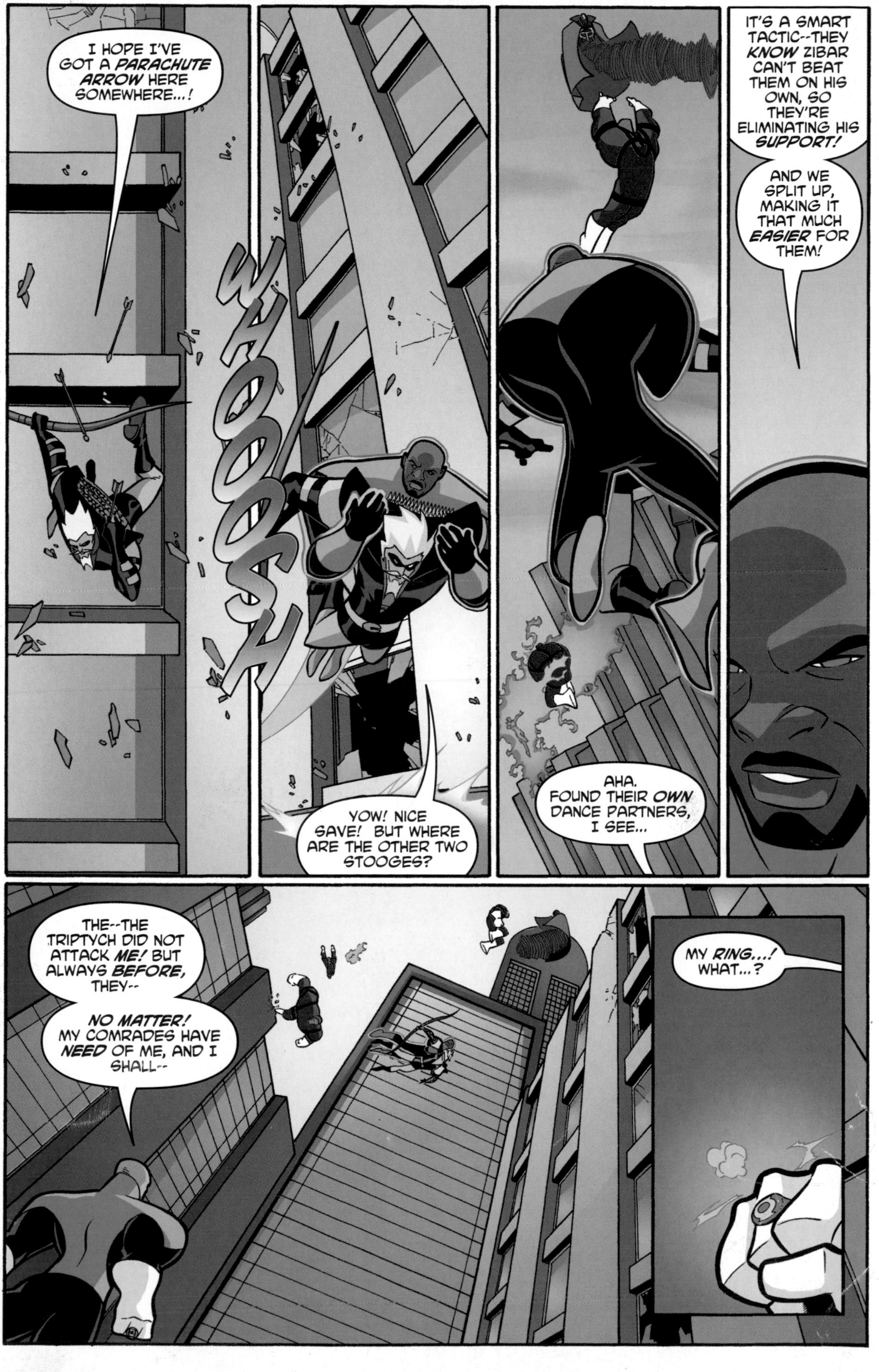
I HOPE I'VE GOT A *PARACHUTE ARROW* HERE SOMEWHERE...!
WHOOOOSH
YOW! NICE SAVE! BUT WHERE ARE THE OTHER TWO STOOGES?
AHA. FOUND THEIR *OWN* DANCE PARTNERS, I SEE...
IT'S A SMART TACTIC--THEY *KNOW* ZIBAR CAN'T BEAT THEM ON HIS OWN, SO THEY'RE ELIMINATING HIS *SUPPORT!*
AND WE SPLIT UP, MAKING IT THAT MUCH *EASIER* FOR THEM!
THE--THE TRIPTYCH DID NOT ATTACK *ME!* BUT ALWAYS *BEFORE,* THEY--
NO MATTER! MY COMRADES HAVE *NEED* OF ME, AND I SHALL--
MY *RING...!* WHAT...?

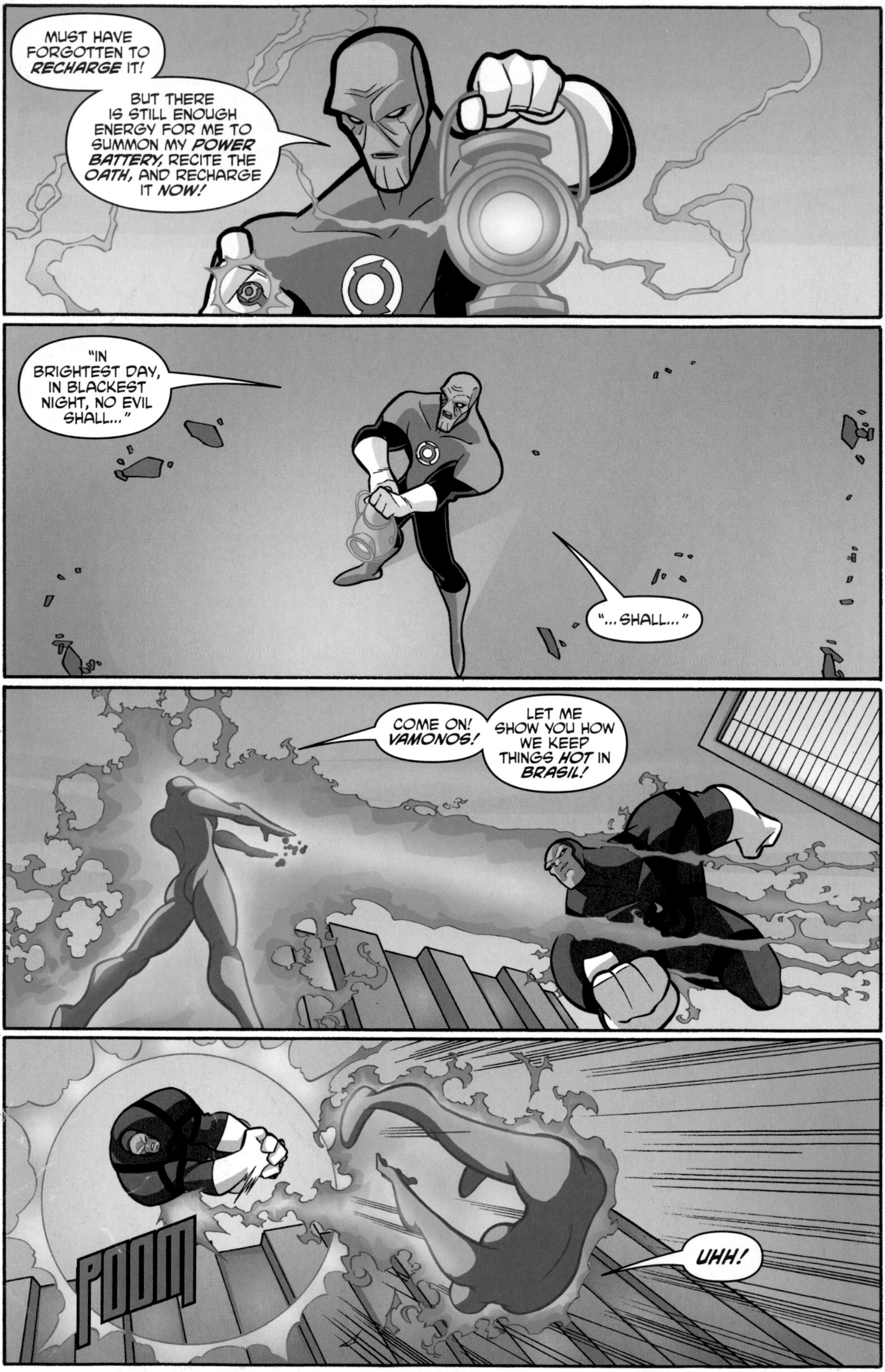
MUST HAVE FORGOTTEN TO RECHARGE IT!
BUT THERE IS STILL ENOUGH ENERGY FOR ME TO SUMMON MY POWER BATTERY, RECITE THE OATH, AND RECHARGE IT NOW!
"IN BRIGHTEST DAY, IN BLACKEST NIGHT, NO EVIL SHALL..."
"...SHALL..."
COME ON! VAMONOS!
LET ME SHOW YOU HOW WE KEEP THINGS HOT IN BRASIL!
POOM
UHH!

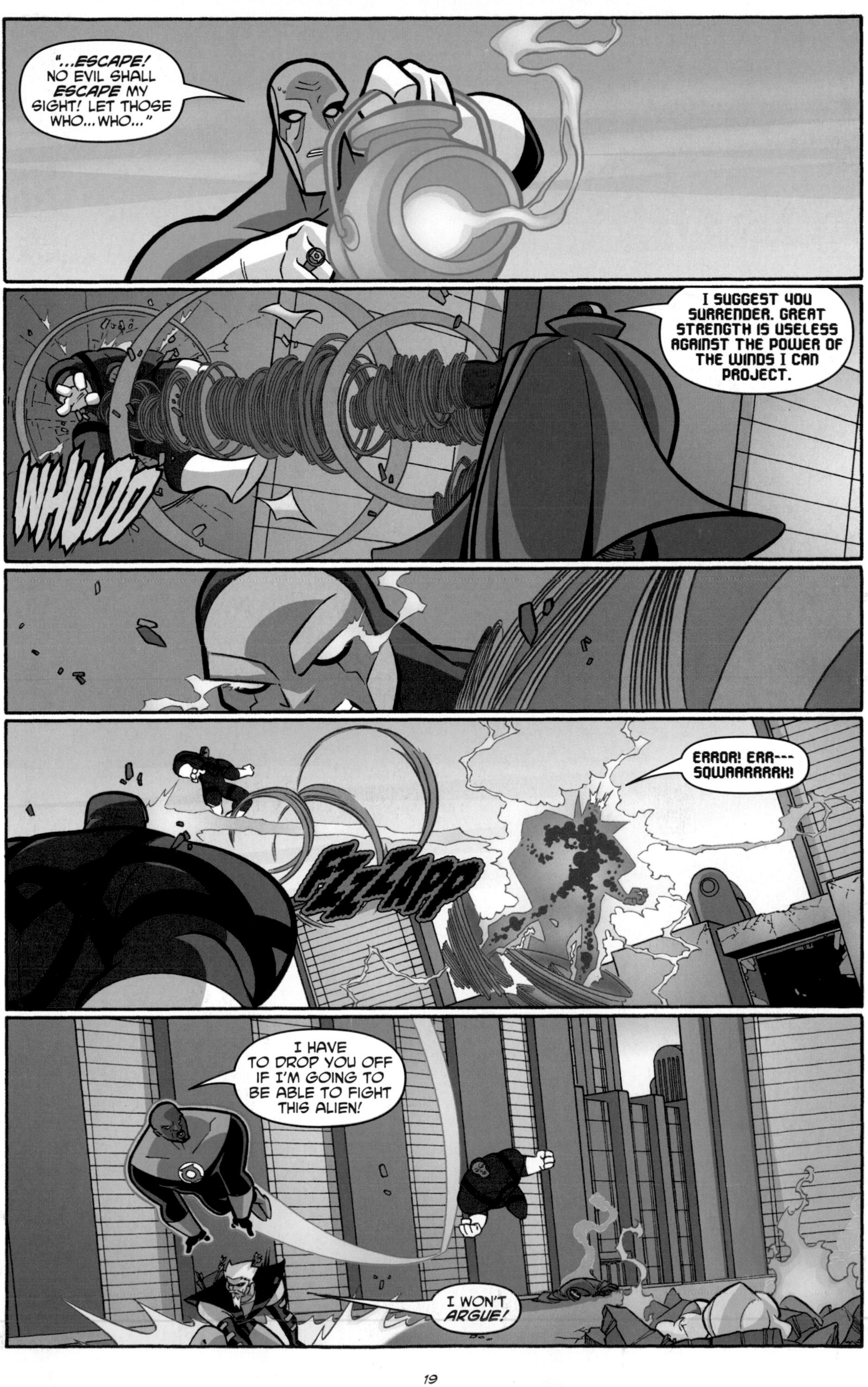
"...ESCAPE! NO EVIL SHALL ESCAPE MY SIGHT! LET THOSE WHO...WHO..."
I SUGGEST YOU SURRENDER. GREAT STRENGTH IS USELESS AGAINST THE POWER OF THE WINDS I CAN PROJECT.
WHUDD
ERROR! ERR--- SQWAARRRRK!
FZZAPP
I HAVE TO DROP YOU OFF IF I'M GOING TO BE ABLE TO FIGHT THIS ALIEN!
I WON'T ARGUE!

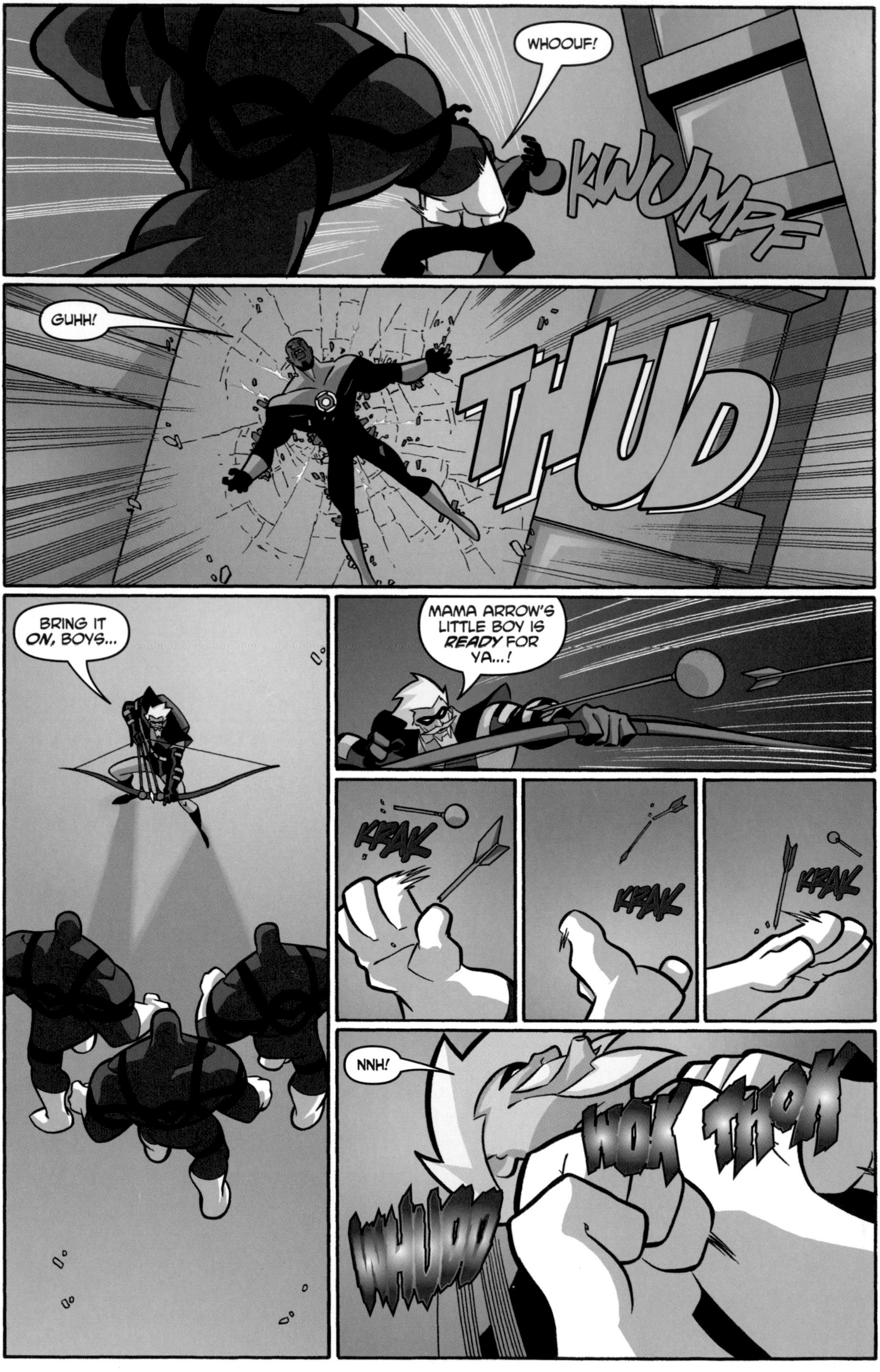
WHOOUF!
KWUMPF
GUHH!
THUD
BRING IT ON, BOYS...
MAMA ARROW'S LITTLE BOY IS READY FOR YA...!
KRAK
KRAK
KRAK
NNH!
WOK
THOK
WHUDD

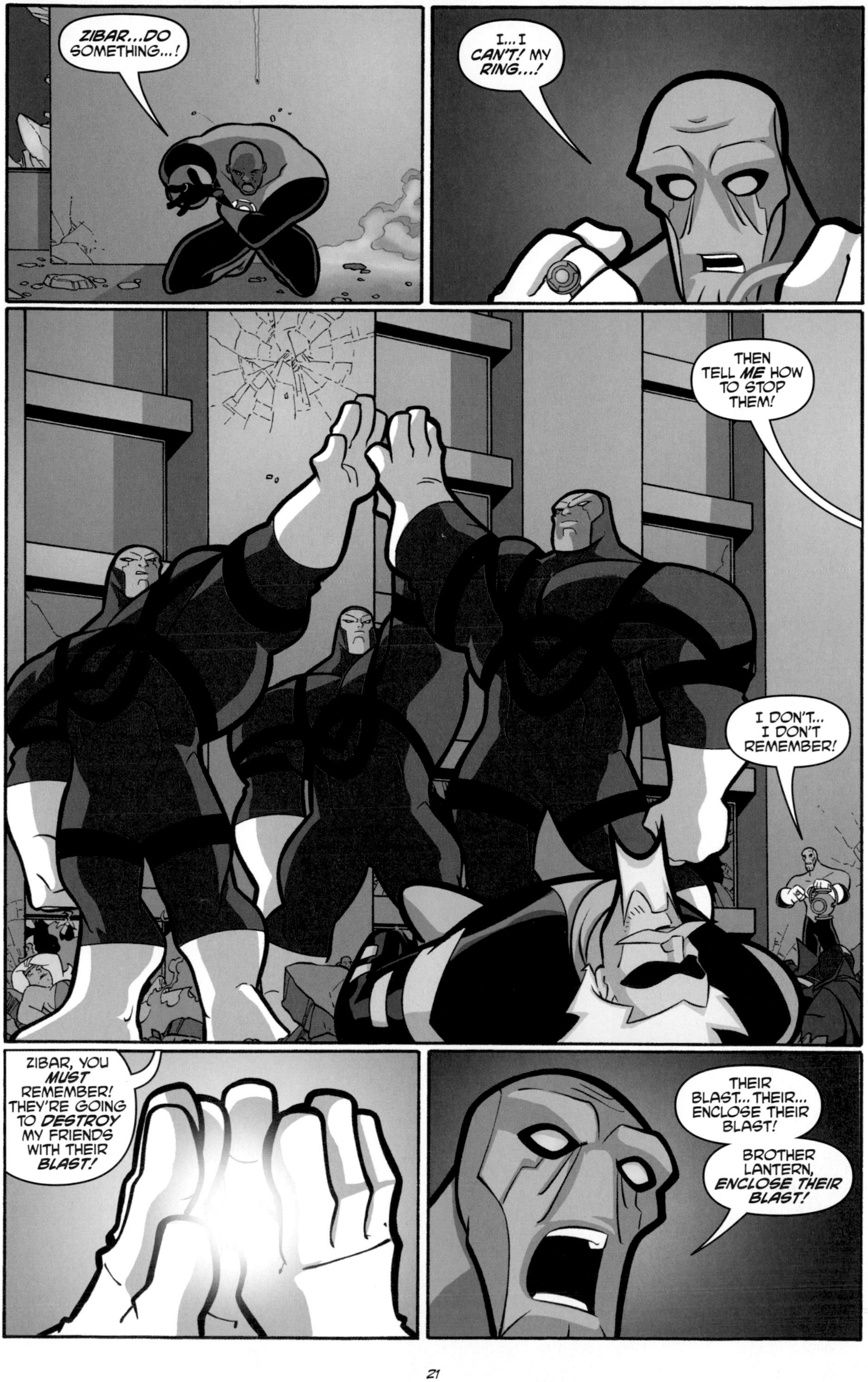
ZIBAR...DO SOMETHING...!
I...I CAN'T! MY RING...!
THEN TELL ME HOW TO STOP THEM!
I DON'T... I DON'T REMEMBER!
ZIBAR, YOU MUST REMEMBER! THEY'RE GOING TO DESTROY MY FRIENDS WITH THEIR BLAST!
THEIR BLAST... THEIR... ENCLOSE THEIR BLAST!
BROTHER LANTERN, ENCLOSE THEIR BLAST!

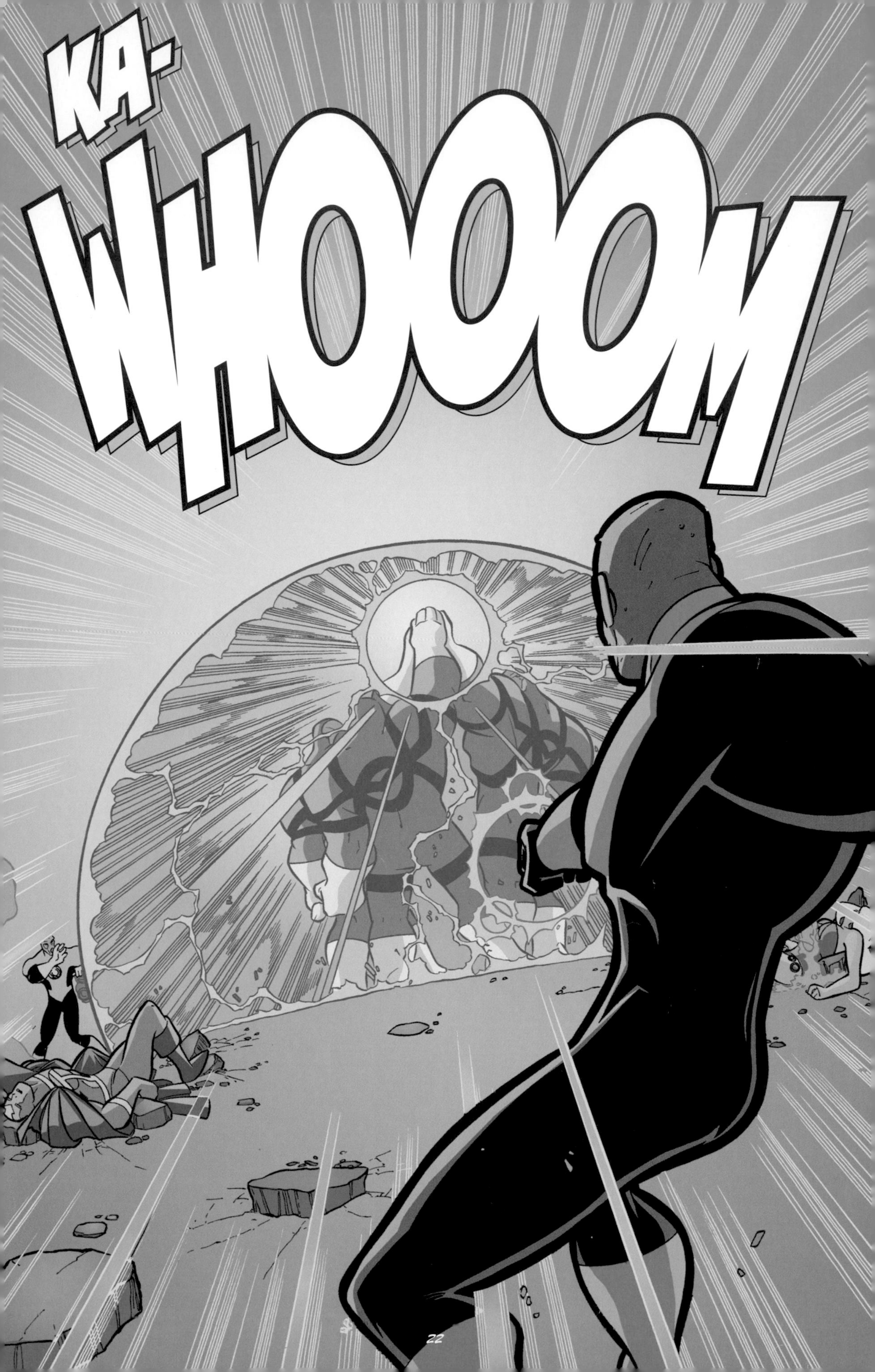
KA-
WHOOOM

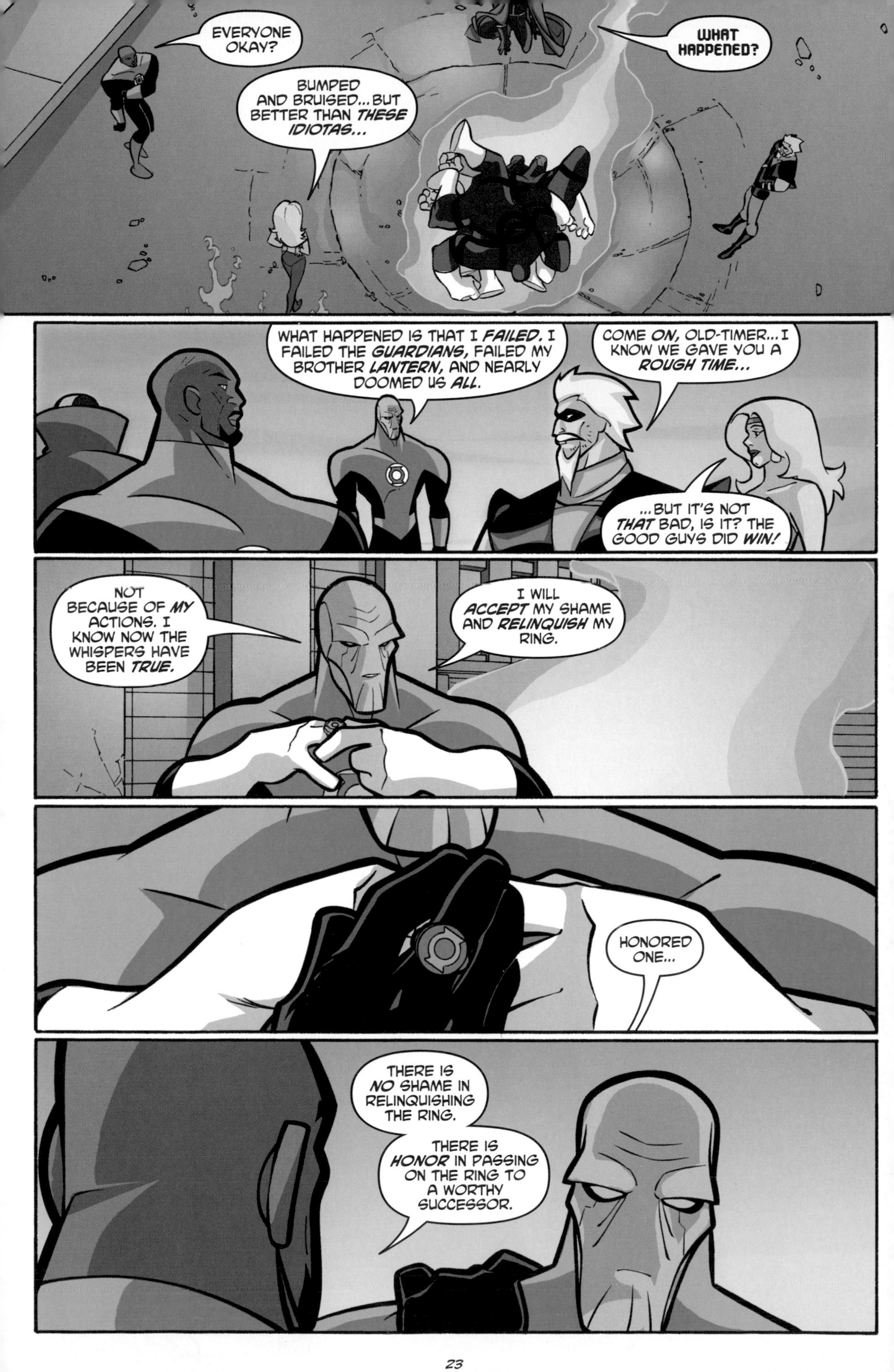
EVERYONE OKAY?
WHAT HAPPENED?
BUMPED AND BRUISED... BUT BETTER THAN THESE IDIOTAS...
WHAT HAPPENED IS THAT I FAILED. I FAILED THE GUARDIANS, FAILED MY BROTHER LANTERN, AND NEARLY DOOMED US ALL.
COME ON, OLD-TIMER... I KNOW WE GAVE YOU A ROUGH TIME...
...BUT IT'S NOT THAT BAD, IS IT? THE GOOD GUYS DID WIN!
NOT BECAUSE OF MY ACTIONS. I KNOW NOW THE WHISPERS HAVE BEEN TRUE.
I WILL ACCEPT MY SHAME AND RELINQUISH MY RING.
HONORED ONE...
THERE IS NO SHAME IN RELINQUISHING THE RING.
THERE IS HONOR IN PASSING ON THE RING TO A WORTHY SUCCESSOR.

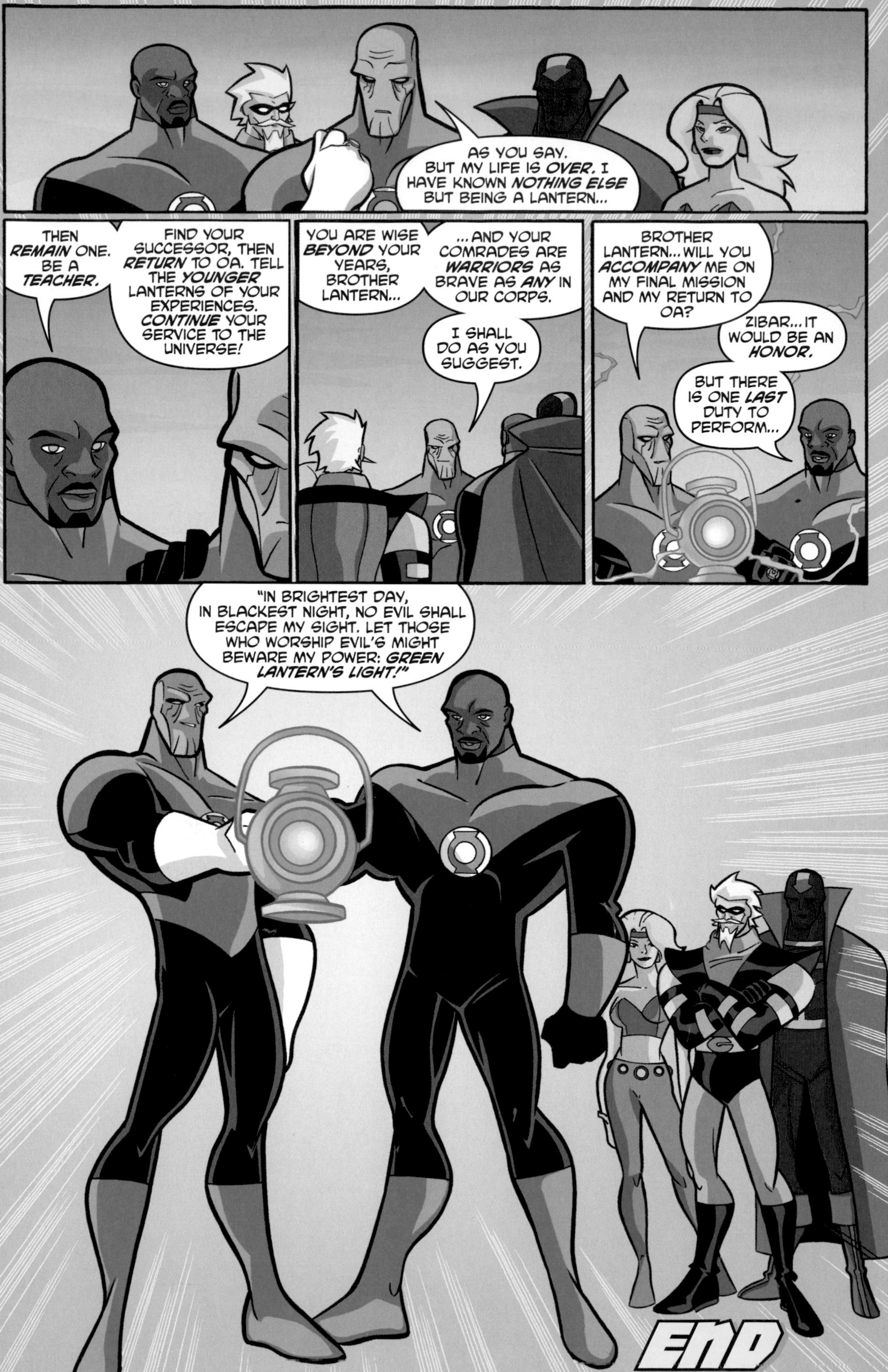
AS YOU SAY. BUT MY LIFE IS OVER. I HAVE KNOWN NOTHING ELSE BUT BEING A LANTERN...
THEN REMAIN ONE. BE A TEACHER.
FIND YOUR SUCCESSOR, THEN RETURN TO OA. TELL THE YOUNGER LANTERNS OF YOUR EXPERIENCES. CONTINUE YOUR SERVICE TO THE UNIVERSE!
YOU ARE WISE BEYOND YOUR YEARS, BROTHER LANTERN...
...AND YOUR COMRADES ARE WARRIORS AS BRAVE AS ANY IN OUR CORPS.
I SHALL DO AS YOU SUGGEST.
BROTHER LANTERN... WILL YOU ACCOMPANY ME ON MY FINAL MISSION AND MY RETURN TO OA?
ZIBAR... IT WOULD BE AN HONOR.
BUT THERE IS ONE LAST DUTY TO PERFORM...
"IN BRIGHTEST DAY, IN BLACKEST NIGHT, NO EVIL SHALL ESCAPE MY SIGHT. LET THOSE WHO WORSHIP EVIL'S MIGHT BEWARE MY POWER: GREEN LANTERN'S LIGHT!"
END

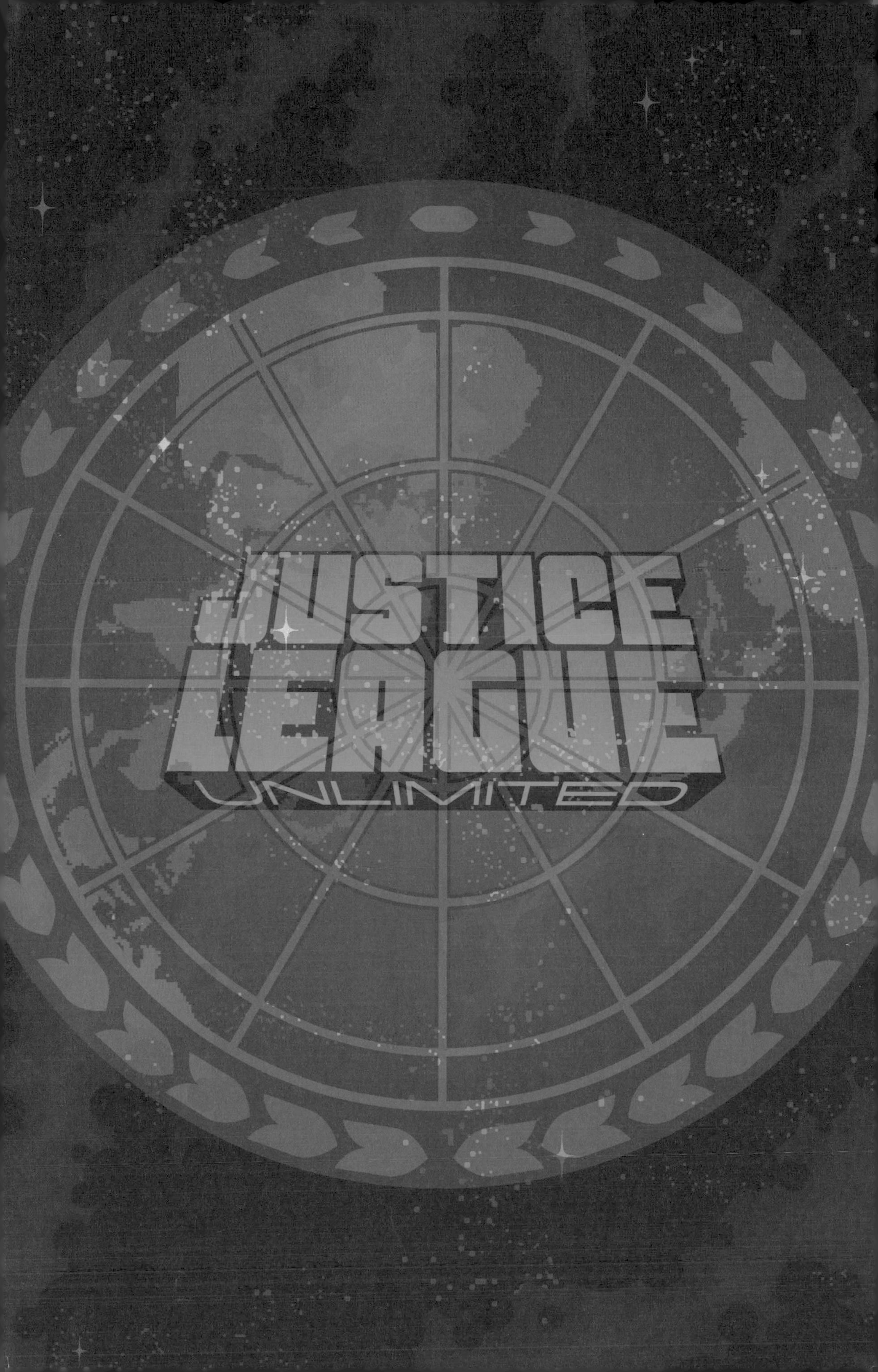
JUSTICE LEAGUE
UNLIMITED

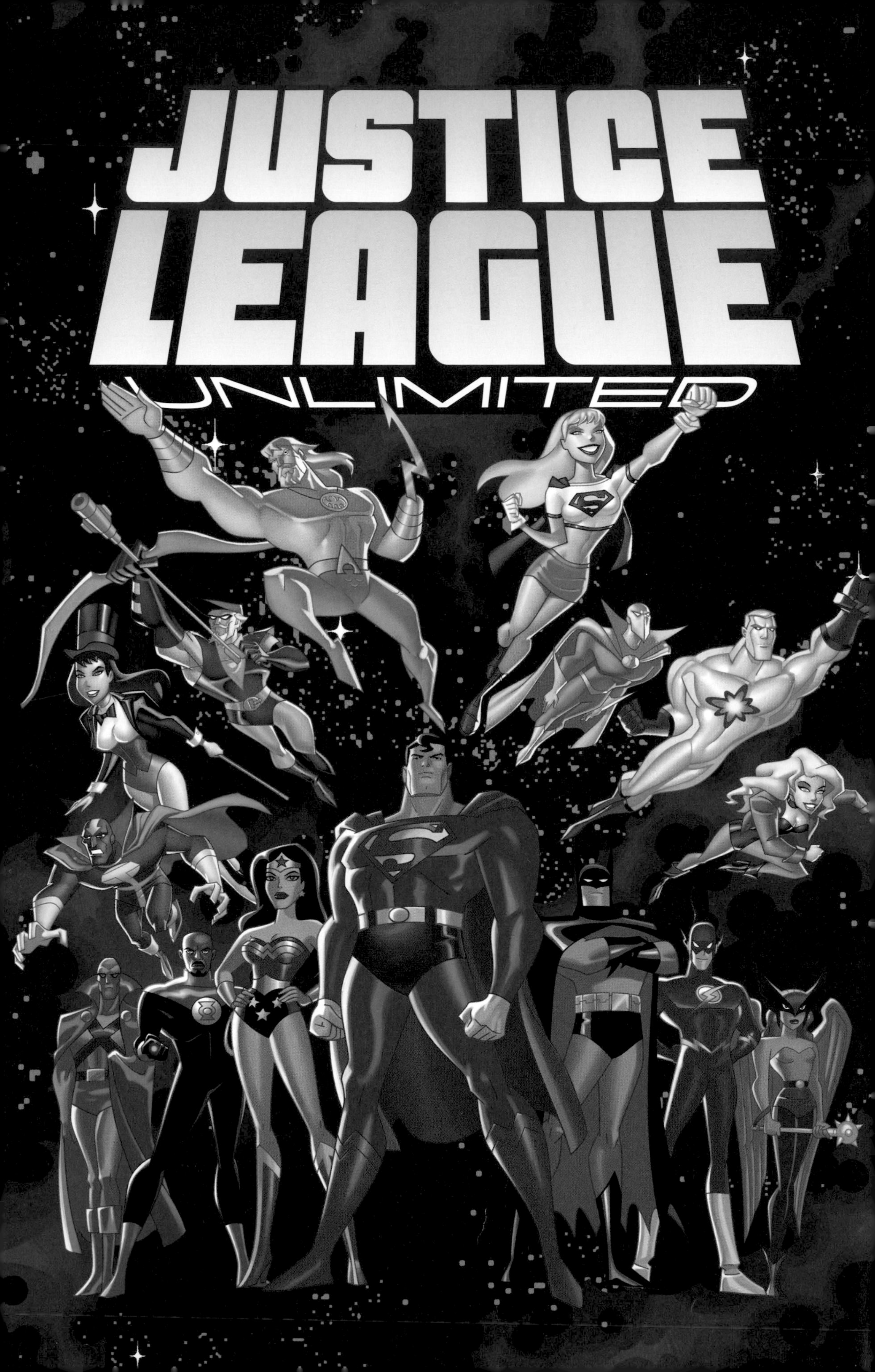
JUSTICE LEAGUE
UNLIMITED

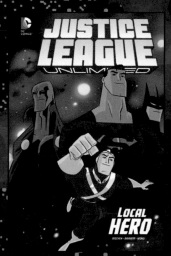

CREATORS

ADAM BEECHEN WRITER

Adam Beechen has written a variety of TV cartoons, including *Ben Ten: Alien Force*, *Teen Titans*, *Batman: The Brave and the Bold*, *The Batman* [for which he received an Emmy nomination], *Rugrats*, *The Wild Thornberrys*, *X-Men: Evolution*, and *Static Shock*, as well as the live-action series *Ned's Declassified School Survival Guide* and *The Famous Jett Jackson*. He is also the author of *Hench*, a graphic novel, and has scripted many comic books, including *Batgirl*, *Teen Titans*, *Robin*, and *Justice League Unlimited*. In addition Adam has written dozens of children's books, as well as an original young adult novel, *What I Did On My Hypergalactic Interstellar Summer Vacation*.

CARLO BARBERI ARTIST

Carlo Barberi is a professional comic book artist from Monterrey, Mexico. His best-known works for DC Comics include *Batman: The Brave and the Bold*, *The Flash*, *Blue Beetle*, *Gen 13*, and *Justice League Unlimited*.

WALDEN WONG ARTIST

Walden Wong is a professional comic book artist, inker, and colorist. He's worked on some of DC Comics' top characters, including Superman, Batman, Wonder Woman, and more.

WORD GLOSSARY

concussive (con-KUHSS-iv)--if something is concussive, it shakes violently or stuns

crisis (KRYE-sis)--a time of danger and difficulty

dispersed (diss-PURSSD)--scattered

enhanced (en-HANSSD)--improved something or raised the value of it

execute (EK-suh-kyoot)--if you execute an order, you put it into action

longitude (LON-juh-tood)--the position of a place, measured in degrees east or west of a line that runs through the Greenwich observatory

mandatory (MAN-duh-tor-ee)--required

relinquish (ri-LING-kwish)--give up or let go

shame (SHAME)--dishonor or disgrace

sufficient (suh-FISH-uhnt)--if something is sufficient, it is enough or adequate

J.L.U. GLOSSARY

TEAR-GAS ARROW

This particular arrow from the Green Arrow's quiver emits a tear gas that bewilders and incapacitates his foes.

POWER RING

Green Lantern's power ring enables him to create light contstructs that move and function just like their real, physical counterparts.

POWER BATTERY

The Green Lantern Corps members use a power battery to charge their power rings.

VISUAL QUESTIONS & PROMPTS

1. Write down a basic summary of what happened in this panel [from page 8], starting with Green Arrow's attack and ending with the result.

2. Based on the surrounding panels on page 11, what kind of device do you think Zidane has created with his power ring in this panel?

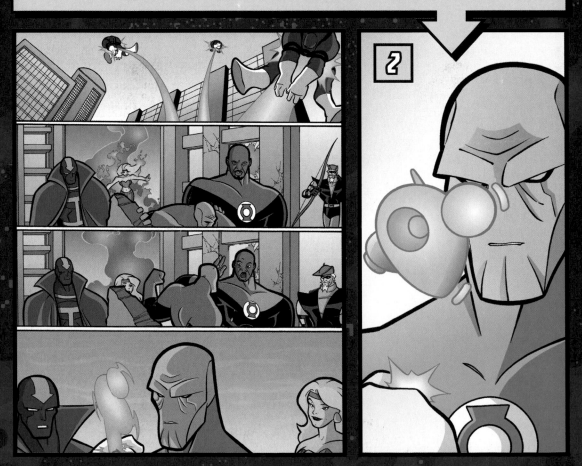

3. Why did the lanterns decide to create a capsule over the Triptych?

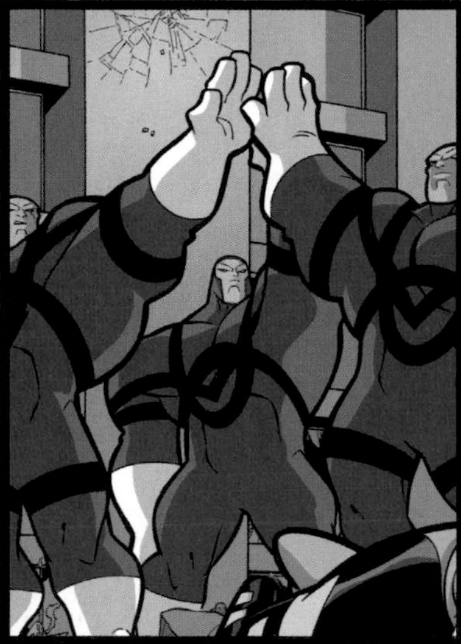

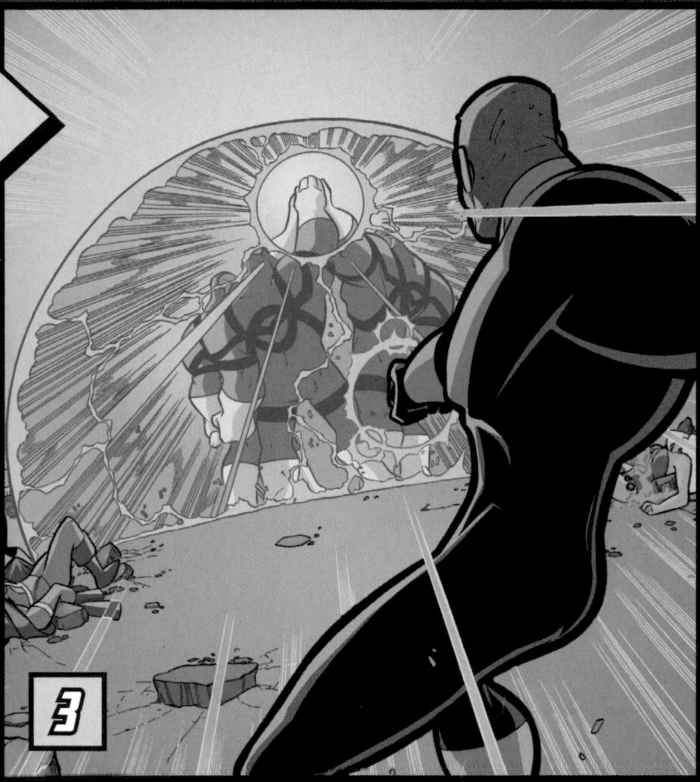
3

4. Based on what you know about Red Tornado from this book, why do you think his speech bubbles look different than the other characters' bubbles?

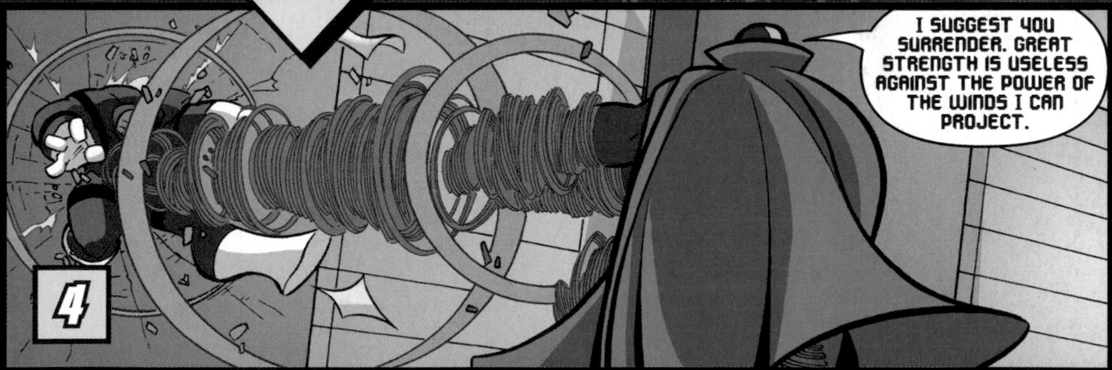
I SUGGEST YOU SURRENDER. GREAT STRENGTH IS USELESS AGAINST THE POWER OF THE WINDS I CAN PROJECT.
4

5. Why did the creators of this comic book choose to add a bright background color in this panel? Read the surrounding panels [on page 21] for clues.

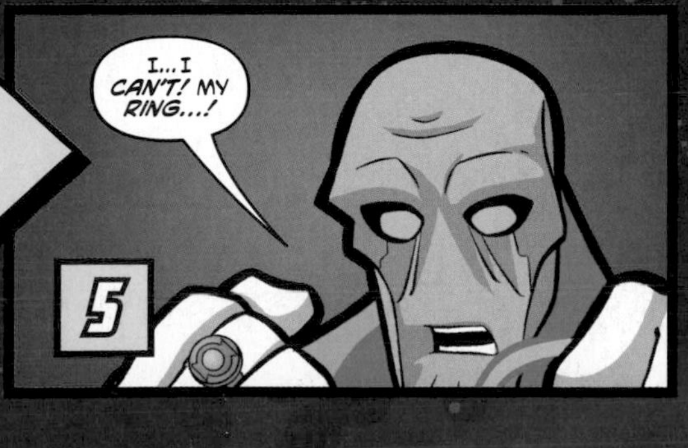
I...I *CAN'T!* MY *RING...!*
5

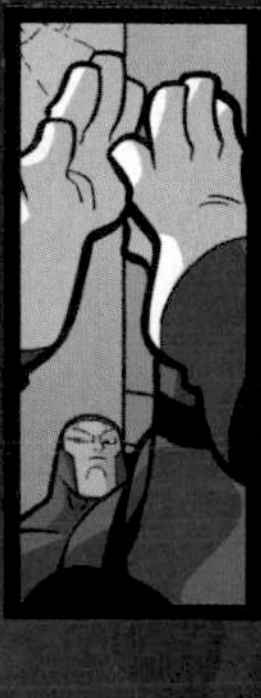

WANT EVEN MORE?

GO TO...

WWW.CAPSTONEKIDS.COM

Then find cool websites and more books like this one at *www.facthound.com.*

Just type in the BOOK ID:
9781434260420